BORDER CROSSINGS

A Minnesota Voices Project Reader

BORDER CROSSINGS

A Minnesota Voices Project Reader

Edited by Jonis Agee, Roger Blakely,
John Rezmerski, Janet Shaw,
and C. W. Truesdale

Graphics by Cherie Doyle and Tracy Turner

 New Rivers Press 1984

Library of Congress Catalog Card Number: 84-060335
ISBN 0-89823-054-3
Book Design by C. W. Truesdale and Daren Sinsheimer
Typesetting by Peregrine Cold Type
Keylining by Daren Sinsheimer

Credits and acknowledgements for material previously published in periodi-
cals can be found in the section called "Notes on Contributors and Acknowledgements," starting on page 283.

New Rivers Press is supported in part by the United Arts Fund with special
assistance from the McKnight Foundation. The publication of *Border Crossings: A Minnesota Voices Project Reader* has been made possible in part by
grants from the National Endowment for the Arts (with funds appropriated
by the Congress of the United States) and by the Dayton Hudson Foundation
with funds provided by *B. Dalton*
BOOKSELLER

New Rivers Press books are distributed by

Bookslinger	and	Small Press Distribution
213 E. 4th St.		1784 Shattuck Ave.
St. Paul, Mn 55101		Berkeley, Ca 94709

Border Crossings: A Minnesota Voices Project Reader has been printed in the
United States of America for New Rivers Press, Inc. (C. W. Truesdale,
editor/publisher) 1602 Selby Ave., St. Paul, MN 55104 in a first edition of
2000 copies.

This anthology is

dedicated to

all those writers who are finding

new borders to cross

BORDER CROSSINGS

GRAPHICS

Tracy Turner

10, 13 Two drawings for Rockcastle's "Memories of a Maria Goretti Girl"
136 Drawing for Roth's "Waitress Journal"

Paul Hansen

154, 156 Drawings for his father's poems

Christopher Hansen

158, 160, 162-6, 168, 170 Drawings for his father's poems

Cherie Doyle

2 "Summer Vessel," 1982 (4 5/8" x 5 3/4"—collage, b/w xerox)
33 "Penny Mask," 1984 (32" x 40"—acrylic)
52 "Rose/Stem," 1983 (29" x 40"—acrylic)
60 "Hay/Fire," 1983-4 (29" x 40"—mixed media)
87 "Woman, 1981 (29" x 40"—acrylic)
96 "Ionic Vessel," 1983 (29" x 44"—acrylic)
120 "Valentine," 1981 (32" x 40"—collage/acrylic)
196 "Little Theatre," 1980 (29" x 40"—acylic/pastels)
    —*Collection of Gail Kendall, St. Paul, MN*
210 "Vase: Still Life," 1980 (32" x 40")—mixed media)
    —*Collection of Steven and Laura Doyle, St. Paul, MN*
220 "Dog/Vase," 1983 (26" x 40")—acrylic)
274 "Guatamelan Still Life," 1982 (8" x 10")—collage, b/w xerox)
282 "Water Roses: Mysteries," 1982 (29" x 44"—mixed media)
    —*Collection of Michael and Maureen Wagner, St. Paul, MN*
Front Cover "Wind Fan," 1984 (26" x 40"—acrylic)

BORDER CROSSINGS

In that long-ago time of myth and legend, an old couple named Baucis and Philemon once opened the door of their poor cottage to a pair of weary travelers. Though their cupboard was bare, they offered these wayfarers the last cupfuls of milk from a pitcher standing on their kitchen table. Miraculously this pitcher never ran dry, no matter how many refills the thirsty guests begged from them.

It was then that the old couple knew they were entertaining gods unaware: Zeus and Hermes in this instance, who praised and rewarded such unexpected generosity.

We judges of the 1983 Minnesota Voices Competition hardly qualify as deities, but we have been entertained splendidly by a miraculous pitcher or urn or treasure-trove of poems and stories—far more than the set of books we published last fall could fairly represent.

This urn continues to overflow. We now offer a sampling of the work of other writers from that competition. You will find poems about the Mississippi, the prairies, the forests, the small towns, the inner city, about growing up, about the heartaches of parenting or maintaining meaningful relationships, about the zest of love and the bitterness of quarrels. You will find stories about young men who want to join monasteries, about older folk trying to keep life from ripping apart in their hands, and about the rites of passage of young women.

Here is a great variety of voices—many of them new and unfamiliar. There was a great deal more in other manuscripts we read and liked but lack the space to print from at this time. The editors felt that a stronger and more cohesive collection would only be possible if we made a generous selection from each author represented.

We now invite our readers to share in this largesse and hope that they will agree with the editors that this anthology testifies to strength and energy of writing in this region.

Each of the five panelists who judged the 1983 Minnesota Voices Competition had a hand in making these selections. It is our hope that *Border Crossings* will become just the first in a series of annual or, at least, bi-annual celebrations.

We are very grateful to the Dayton Hudson Foundation and especially to B. Dalton, Bookseller for their foresight in underwriting this anthology.

— *Jonis Agee*
  Roger Blakely
  John Rezmerski
  Janet Shaw
  C. W. Truesdale

BORDER CROSSINGS

A Minnesota Voices Project Reader

Mary Francois Rockcastle

MEMORIES OF A MARIA GORETTI GIRL

During Lent Liza knelt in the darkened church to say the stations. After school when it was so quiet and you could smell the incense from Novena, she became certain that someday she'd be a saint. Hadn't Monsignor given her the prize for the best essay in the class—"What Sacrifice Means to Me?" She remembered the darkness in the attic where she'd gone to write. The cross hung against the wall and its blood filled the dusty Christmas ornament boxes. She had no right to be so selfish and proud and the thought of true sacrifice filled her heart. When Sister collected the essays, hers was the longest and she knew as she turned it in that she would win. The humility of the cross had done it.

At dinner Matt annouced he was giving up chocolate for Lent. Her father patted his shoulder.

"And what about you, James?"

James shuffled his feet. He hadn't given up anything.

"It's silly giving up something."

"What kind of answer is that?"

"It's the truth. All this sacrifice talk, who's it helping, anyway?"

"You can tell the priest that in confession, James." Her mother pinched his neck hard. They looked at her next. She was the youngest but already the most holy.

"I'm going to daily Mass, and Novenas every Wednesday."

The boys ate without looking up. Neither of them had even entered the sacrifice contest and her winning had driven them away.

The girl scout troop had scheduled the auditorium for 3:10 p.m. Liza hurried down the dark stairs with her friends. The younger girls sat in the back, where they couldn't see well. Mrs. Sheehan turned the light off and Liza's row swooned with a concerted gasp because two eighth grade boys had remained in the room to operate the projector.

M-E-N-S-T-R-U-A-T-I-O-N Colorful diagrams moved and leaked

across the screen as the modulated male voice explained the awesome process. Sperm swam up rivers, eggs dropped lazily down long tubes, the acorn blossomed and grew and the voice spoke the word pregnant. Liza winced that the boys also saw the waves of red washing over the screen. Her mother called it the curse and wore diapers when she first got it.

After the film Mrs. Sheehan explained about the eggs and something about marriage and babies. The older girls asked questions and Liza wanted to be the first in the row to ask.

"Mrs. Sheehan, how do the eggs know you're married?"

She stormed down the basement steps to where her mother was washing clothes. She'd been betrayed and the knowledge filled her with rage. All the talking and still she didn't know.

"They laughed at me!" Her mother flipped on the dryer switch and turned around.

"All the girls. They laughed when I asked how the eggs knew." She began to cry.

"Liza, what are you talking about?"

"Menstruation. Mrs. Sheehan said after you were married the egg got pregnant. You never told me the egg knew."

Her mother stared, the blue eyes innocent and concerned.

"Liza, the sperm comes from a man." Then she told her the rest. Sweet Jesus, no. Say it's not true. And if the other girls knew that when she asked the question. Her mother and father. Mr. and Mrs. Sheehan. In bed at night under the covers. It was too horrible to think about.

After Novena she waited for the people to leave so she would be alone with the stained glass window above the altar. The resurrected Christ opened his arms and light shone from the wounds. She stared at it until the white robe blurred and the yellow glow made her tremble with love. For she knew if she knelt in the aisle and stretched out her arms to him, he would take her up, like he'd done to Saint Thérèse, the little flower. She need only wait for the right time to do it. He would send a signal and she prayed that it be during one of these private times and not on Sunday when the church was full. Because she feared she might not have the courage to get up then in front of everyone and kneel in the aisle with her hands outspread and reaching for Christ.

The cat chewed her zipper and Liza pinched it against her body to keep her grip on the tree. Matt shimmied up the long part without branches. She hooked her arms and legs around the trunk like he'd done but couldn't get more than a few inches.

"I can see Washington's rock." Matt's knife caught the sun as he whittled his initials in the top of the tree.

The cat wailed and Liza pulled its claws from her coat. A yellow stream squirted down the front of her jacket. She let go. Branches whipped it as the cat clawed for safety on the way down. The thud and whining scream brought them scrambling down the tree.

"Don't be afraid, Kitty. I didn't mean to drop you." She smelled the urine on her coat.

"Let's go play in the barn." Matt slung the cat under his arm and they walked to the old barn in back of Fisher's lot. Upstairs, Liza took the whimpering cat from Matt and lay it in the hay. It was dark and the bales looked big. Matt uncovered a cardboard box and put the cat in it. He found pieces of frayed rope and tied them together to make a harness for the box.

"We'll give it elevator rides out the window." They hung out the window and lowered the box. The cat scratched the sides and tried to jump out, meowing as the box carried it up and down. The smell of urine and feces increased as they pulled the box close to them and the cat's scream was all she heard. Liza's hand burned as they pulled the rope faster and faster. Her head rocked and she could hardly breathe. The rope snapped, and the box tilted, the cat grasping at the line still intact. Its yellow eyes circled insanely and it hit the ground hard.

She and Matt held the box, which dangled from one line. The cay lay like a pretzel and made no sound. Leaves dragged along the ground and Mrs. Whalen with the gimp leg stopped by the cat. Gently she picked it up and cradled it in her thin arms. Matt pulled back when she looked up. Then she turned and limped back through the woods to her house.

"Come on, Liza, let's beat it."

He pulled her down the steps and across Fisher's yard until the barn was out of sight. They lay on the grass, not touching.

"Did you see that cat hit the ground!"

"Do you think it's dead?"

"Nah, cat's got nine lives."

"Mrs. Whalen'll probably tell Mom and Dad."

"Dad hates cats."

"Mom'll kill us."

"Wait till she sees the pee all over your coat." As he ran off, she yelled after him, "It was your idea!"

In the bathroom she soaked the front of her coat in lysol. Please, sweet Jesus, don't let the kitty die. Don't let it be crippled. O Virgin Mother, let it live and every day I'll say a rosary.

For days Liza waited by the barn, not wanting to go too near Mrs. Whalen's yard, hoping for sight of the kitty. She sat in the leaves and listened to the cooing of the pigeons that crowded the eaves of the Fisher's cupola. It was the tallest house in the neighborhood, and you could always see white droppings on the gray paint. The house molted feathers which the kids on the block collected for Indian bonnets. The constant cooing put her to sleep.

Voices woke her. They were behind the barn, older boys' voices, probably the two Fisher boys and their friends. Bodies thudded against the wall and she heard sharp blows. A cooing choked into a strangled screech, and Liza stood up, her heart thumping. Someone laughed, and there was another blow. She inched close to the wall and waited at the edge, where the side wall joined the back. They were less than two feet away and the scuffling of leaves and sneakers almost touched her. Quickly she jerked her head out and saw it. Ben and Harry Fisher held the squirming pigeon while Lee Phillips swung a hatchet into the bird's white stomach. The metal shaft split the soft feathers into a black seam and blood bubbled out over the white front.

Liza ran from the barn, leaving a piece of her blouse on the fence between Fisher's yard and hers. Matt swerved his bicycle to avoid knocking her down as she ran across the driveway. She sunk on the porch steps and put her head between her knees.

"What the hell's the matter with you?"

When she raised her head, Matt's face doubled and swam.

"Liza, what's wrong?"

"The pigeons." She pointed to the barn. "The Fisher boys are chopping up the pigeons."

"Jesus Christ." He whistled between his teeth and looked with her at the barn. Then he handed her a piece of gum.

"Well, Liza, now you don't have to feel so bad about that dumb cat."

James had a compulsion for accidents which rarely left him intact. At three years old he set himself on fire with a candle from his birthday cake and it left red scars on his arm. A bee bite on his inner thigh bothered him so much he scratched it until the doctors had to open up the leg and insert a drain to get the infection out. During that visit they discovered a half-healed gash on his knee that was so deep they put several stitches in it.

But his head got it the worst. In the first accident he tilted his chair during dinner and with a misplaced kick sent it backwards onto the fireplace. His scalp opened on the stone ledge. Another year he went sledding with his friend, Frankie Ferraro, who couldn't steer well and rode his sled over the top of James' head. It split an artery, and the blood soaked into the snow. Liza felt guilty for the third accident because she pushed him. She, James and Frankie went swimming in the pond near their house and James wore a life preserver because it helped him bounce when he jumped off the dock into the water. Frankie jumped in first and was still under water when Liza pushed James on top of him. A metal hook from the preserver caught between James' chin and Frankie's head. They bobbed in the water, crying, and Liza saw the skin flap under James' chin.

At ten James talked of death in a way that made her father call the priest. They had several sessions in the living room, which she and Matt watched from behind the railing on the darkened stairs.

"What's all this I hear about death, James?"

"You've heard it too, then?"

The priest and her parents exchanged looks.

"No, I didn't hear anything. Your father says you've been talking too much about death."

"What's wrong with that?"

"Well, for a boy your age, death could be very frightening."

"Why?"

The priest shifted in his seat.

"What do you think about death, James?"

"It depends where you go. Maybe I'm chosen for something because I'm always in the emergency room. Mom says it's a cross that only special people get who God loves the most. Then I don't mind it. But I wouldn't want to go to hell and have my head buried in the fire and my feet sticking up out of the circle like a manhole in the ground where snakes would come and curl around my legs."

Liza ran down the stairs into the living room.

"It's the Dante book. The one of Daddy's. James is always looking at the pictures."

She took the big book from the shelf and found the page where Pope Leo was pictured with his head in the ground.

"Here's my favorite."

In Purgatorio she found the page where the greedy suffered. Their pale, skeletal bodies bent twistedly under long slabs of rock they carried on their shoulders.

"Liza, go upstairs."

"Ask him about the French Revolution."

"Go upstairs."

She rejoined Matt on the landing while Father Murphy asked James what he knew about the French Revolution.

"In the movie, when the man was waiting by the guillotine to get his head chopped off, I knew just how he felt. It was like I'd been there before. I even recognized the people standing in the square. When the head came off, I could still see them. A little girl with a white scarf and purple scar on her neck stared at me through the whole thing. I think it must be reincarnation, and that's why I have so many accidents. In every life they'll be trying to sew me up but I keep coming back."

"James, Catholics don't believe in reincarnation."

"Can you prove it, Father?"

Now he'd really be in trouble, since her parents said never to question the priest. Then her father said something to James and he came upstairs. Liza and Matt followed him to his room.

"Did you get it?"

"Get what? All they want now is my notebook."

"James, you better not. Tell them you lost it." Matt put his hand on the notebook James kept in his top drawer.

"Why should I? What's wrong with my notebook? I copied all the pictures from the Inferno and you said yourself they were pretty good."

"Yeah, but the others, James."

"What's *wrong* with them?" He flung off Matt's hand and walked out of the room. Downstairs, Liza heard them turn the pages. When her mother gave a little cry, Liza knew they'd gotten to the pictures in the back. She laughed when James first showed them to her. A preying mantis with James' big ears and blue eyes, holding a drawing pencil and writing in a notebook that said "James' pictures, do not touch." James' face staring from a disembodied head while the executioner dribbled saliva over him. A Viking warrior with James' pigeon toes. He'd drawn a picture of Saint Teresa of Avila being tortured on the wheel and she had his face.

When he came upstairs, he slammed the door of his room. Liza crawled up to his bed.

"What'd they do to you, James?"

"Get out of here."

"Come on, James, tell me."

"Father Murphy took away my notebook. Told me to say a couple of rosaries and not to talk about reincarnation anymore."

"If Father says it's not true, James."

"How does *he* know? In my mythology book, the gods and goddesses turned into trees and fountains and whirlpools and stars and all kinds of things. Just look through a telescope sometime. The Catholics don't know everything, Liza."

"James, you should be ashamed."

"Leave me alone."

After that night, James never showed her his notebooks, which he kept in a drawer with a combination lock. During Mass his eyes wandered and she knew he never paid any attention. Every night before bed, she said a rosary for his soul.

Her mother's full name was Nora Theresa Knowland. The Knowland came from her marriage and was English, which she never let Liza's father forget. "The dirty English," her grandmother Herlihy called them, and fed Liza with tales of the famine and the poor Irish immigrants who came to the American melting pot, those that survived the crossing, only to meet more discrimination but at least it was a chance to live. Not like the starving ones left behind to die.

"Were you born to Ireland, Nanny?"

"No, but my mother was. In the little house kept now by that filthy second cousin. Who shouldn't be there anyway since the inheritance is rightfully mine."

Behind the rheumy white of the growing cataracts, her blue eyes shone. Liza sat next to her mother, whose rare silence gave the old woman space to remember.

"What would you do with the house, Nanny?"

"There's no way you would ever live in it, Mom."

"Not the point! It was my *mother's* house. So it is not right that some second cousin who never even knew my mother should have it."

When she got like that, there was nothing anybody could do. Her mother put on the John McCormack records and the two women listened to the songs and wept. Liza tried to warn her father when he came in, but it was too late.

"Are you listening to that stuff again."

"Is that all you can ever say? That stuff?"

"Oh, Jesus."

"Don't 'Oh Jesus' me! When my grandparents were being starved out of Ireland, where were your ancestors then? Cromwell! He's part of your ancestry, the beast!"

She was still at it when he went down to the basement. Liza sat by the work bench while he whittled the leg of a chair.

"Don't mind Mom, Dad. You know she doesn't mean it."

He patted her arm. "I know, Liza."

"Where were your grandparents born, Daddy?"

"I don't know. My father died when I was so young I could never ask him. And my mother didn't care about those things."

"Are you sure there's no Irish anywhere in your family? It would mean alot to Mom."

He laughed, and because he didn't do that often, she moved closer to him.

"Tell me again about the first time you met Mom."

He looked up from the chair, and in the silence John McCormack's tenor voice trembled through the room. *I'll take you home again, Kathleen.* He winced and made a fist at the ceiling.

"Come on, Dad, tell me. Don't listen to the music."

Across the ocean wild and wide.

"When I first saw your mother, she was the most beautiful girl in the room. Long brown hair that curled round her face, and the bluest eyes I'd ever seen."

To where your heart will feel no pain.

"Then what? Come on, Dad?"

Since first you were my bonnie bride. The roses all have left your cheeks.
"I didn't know how Irish she was then. Turn off that damn music, Nora!"
I've watched them fade away and die.
"Dirty English." Her grandmother mumbled past the cellar door.

For weeks before Christmas she asked her mother to buy her nylon stockings. How could she sing in the choir at Midnight Mass and walk up the aisle with her red candle and be the only girl in the class with socks on and not stockings? Her father looked up from his paper and the boys left the room in disgust.

"Nora, why don't you get the kid stockings?"

Her mother's embarrassed look gave Liza hope. The next day she found a pair of stockings on the bed. Liza hugged them and draped them over her face to smell the synthetic freshness. Then she realized there was no way to hold them up.

"No, I won't buy you a garter belt. Here's some elastic. Just roll it around the tops."

They bagged round her knees and ankles, no matter how tight she sewed them. She went to Woolworth's and bought thicker elastic but that too didn't work. She was frantic and sent her mother long, hateful stares meant to crush her into remorse. On Christmas Eve morning she took the elastic and pinned strips from the tops of the nylons to her undershirt. It worked and the feeling of victory made her fell womanly and strong.

In the choir the girls sang, their high voice filtering through the crowded church. Liza leaned forward to take the strain of the elastic off her shoulders. Then she saw the long runs the pins had made down the front of her stockings. The narrow aisle stretched endlessly and she could see the heads turn to stare at her legs as she walked to the alter. She clenched her fists at her mother's back. A push on her arm made her find her place in the hymn. Then the signal came from the sacristy and the girls filed downstairs. At the back of the church they lined up. The pain seared her shoulders and she tried to loosen the elastic. Another run sped down her leg and her hands grew clammy. One by one, Father Murphy shut off the church lights.

"Liza, straighten up." Clara Hendricks nudged her from behind.

It was worse than death and the only relief was that the dark might hide the runs. The choirmaster lit their red candles. "Straighten up," he hissed at her.

They took small steps up the aisle, the red candles lighting their faces. Liza's hand shook as the straps of her undershirt cut deeper into the flesh. The candle left red drips on the floor after her. "*O come, o come, Emmanuel. And ransom captive Israel.*" Her teeth clamped in her determination not to give in. The blur of people moved by until her father's face told her everyone must know. By this time there were murmurs from those near the aisle and the singing faltered as the girls around her wondered at her crippled shuffle. "*Rejoice, rejoice, O Israel. To thee shall come Immanuel.*" For a moment the flight of the song relieved the pain and she gazed lovingly at the child in the manger.

At the altar Matt's big eyes stared from the black and white altar boy's uniform.

"Straighten up, you moron."

The choirmaster let them sit while they finished the hymns, and she felt his eyes on her legs as she hunched forward. When her mother came up for communion, she looked at Liza with pity and remorse. Liza was glad and wanted her to suffer. Her life was ruined and she prayed to the Virgin to let her shoulders last until the end of the Mass. "*Silent night, holy night.*" Heroically she struggled to walk upright as the girls began their departure down the aisle. "*All is calm, all is bright.*" Through the sweat fogging her eyes, she could see her family and felt the tap of comfort James gave her as she passed. It must be awful if even he felt sorry for her. She would have to run away to a convent since there was no where else to go and it would be impossible to face the choir after vacation.

The day after Christmas her mother laid a garter belt and new pair of stockings on the bed. They took the old stockings and undershirt filled with holes and threw them in the garbage. On New Year's Day Liza pulled the nylons and garter belt from their plastic and wore them under a black velvet skirt her mother had made, in secret, as a present. The choir gathered round the manger and sang for the Christ Child, dropping coins for the needy in the sweet hay.

Monsignor had established the Maria Goretti club years before Liza went to St. Anne's. It was an honor to belong and all the girls waited expectantly for Monsignor to hand out the Maria Goretti books. Liza read it in her room. Over and over she read the description of Maria's stabbing by the village boy her family had taken in to work in the fields during harvest. He wanted to rape her but she held him off so he stabbed her twenty four times. In the ambulance she clutched a crucifix while her mother wept. They could not keep her alive there were so many wounds so she lay in a coffin in her white communion dress. Liza vowed to be pure to the memory of Maria Goretti.

That year Monsignor brought Maria Goretti's brother to St. Anne's to talk to the club. He was on a tour from Italy and it was an honor to have him visit. Liza listened reverently as the old man spoke to them about his sister. Suddenly he stopped and pointed to her. Monsignor asked Liza to stand while Mr. Goretti tearfully told the class how much she looked like the dead Maria. Her heart froze and the girls looked at her in admiration. She was elected Maria Goretti of the month and won a special silver pin.

At night the street light shone on her ceiling and she knew it was the Holy Ghost. She thanked him for sending the sign but prayed he not appear to her. She was afraid her heart might stop.

Liza and Monica Smith played in Monica's room on Saturday mornings. They dressed up in scarfs and turbans and pretended they were harem women. Monica gave her rolled-up socks and they stuffed them under the scarfs which they wrapped around their tiny breasts. Liza lay on the floor and Monica leaned over her and rubbed the bulging scarf and they pretended to make love. They felt each other's nipples and kissed on the lips.

That week Liza asked her father to go to St. Bernard's to confession instead of St. Anne's.

"Why St. Bernard's?"

"Just for a change, Dad. St. Anne's always has Bingo and the confessions get crowded when the priests take their breaks."

If they went to St. Anne's, Father Murphy would know it was her. Her father took her to St. Bernard's where Liza whispered to the priest that she'd done something "bad" with her friend.

"What did you do?"

"Oh, well, not much really. We dressed up in her mother's clothes."

"What else did you do?"

She didn't know how to tell him. The gas in her stomach hurt and she had to hold it to ease the pain.

"Well, I guess we didn't do anything bad. We were playing that we were grown-ups and married."

"What did you do?"

If only he'd stop asking questions. She'd confessed it already and if that was what mattered, he should just give her the penance.

"We touched each other. Oh, just forget it." She ran out of the confessional and knelt in the back of the church to wait for her father. In the morning she wrote a note that she was going to early Mass by herself. She walked the two miles so they wouldn't see she hadn't gone to Communion. They'd question her since they knew she'd been to confession and there was no way she could tell them why she'd left the confessional before getting the penance.

Because she got the highest marks in English, Sister Donna gave her the biography of Theresa Newman who was a stigmatic. The book had pictures of Therese in her garden looking at her hands which bled from wide-open wounds. Every Lent they opened and she was confined to her bed while the agony lasted. People came to the house to see it, but the priest and nurses kept them away. Her family prayed in the living room and changed the blood-soaked sheets daily. The lashes on her back left red slats like blinds on the sheet and they rubbed her forehead where the crown of thorns had torn the skin. She was up for sainthood and Liza prayed that the three miracles needed come soon so she could pray to Theresa Newman. Matt and James came to her room and together they looked at the pictures. James couldn't stand to look and said she was a quack and he and Matt fought over Theresa Newman's honor. Finally it was all she talked about and could describe the ordeal word for word from the book so her mother took it away and told Sister Donna not to give her any more books like that.

Of all the "fast" girls, Liza most admired Holly McDougal. In 7th grade Holly teased her red hair into a beehive and caked liquid makeup over her freckles. She pinned up the hem of her uniform skirt to show her knees and refused to wear the regulation blouse. As Liza's starched, Peter Pan collar scratched her neck, she stared at the soft, freckled breasts pressing through Holly's v-necked blouse. Every morning the class waited for Sister George's crooked finger, beckoning Holly into the hall. Through the door Sister George's black head shook over Holly's cakey face, eyes stuck to the tile ceiling.

On the mornings Liza knelt in church, Holly slept late and arrived tardy. When the class went to Mass on First Fridays, Holly leaned back during consecration and picked the dirt from her nails. Kneeling next to her, Liza bowed her head and pressed a balled fist against the navy bodice of her uniform.

When it was her turn in speech class, Holly walked slowly to the front of the room, turned her head to the window and spoke to the trees: "My name is Holly McDougal. My parents are divorced, the nuns hate me, and I hate their lover, Jesus Christ." In the room's hush Sister George rustled like a flock of birds as she moved up the aisle to stand beside Holly. Tall and thin in her black, she reached for Holly's chin and cupped it in her long fingers.

"You leave this room now, Holly McDougal, and never come back."

Without looking at anyone, Holly passed through the door. The next day she was absent and the day after that Father Murphy came to the door during class and took Sister out in the hall. When she returned, her face stared whitely from her black and she told the class that Holly McDougal was dead. Although lessons continued, she didn't raise her voice all that day.

In the playground at lunch, Monica Smith ran from the rectory where her mother worked and told the girls what her mother had overheard in the priest's dining room.

"Her boyfriend—the one in the apartment—shot her through the heart. He kept a gun in his bureau. The hospital called Father Murphy to give her Extreme Unction but she died on the operating table before he got there."

It was her first wake and she feared seeing the dead body. Matt and James treated her with respect as neither of them had ever been to a wake. Over and over she imagined the gunshot wound and what Holly had felt before she died. If she'd had any time to think or had just blacked out. If, finally, she'd feared going to hell, or had said an Act of Contrition. Her mother took her to the wake and they waited in line for twenty minutes before they entered the room where Holly was. All the kids came to pay their respects to the dead. When they stood alongside the coffin, Liza pulled away. The red hair was combed flat off her face, not even a tease, and the pale skin was dusted with freckles. They'd dressed her in the school uniform and regulation blouse which lay flat on her sunken chest. White rhinestone rosary beads wrapped round her folded hands and made rainbows on the satin walls of the casket. It wasn't even Holly anymore. To bury her in the uniform she hated, without a curl in her hair or rouge on her cheeks. It was cruel and there was nothing sacred about it. Liza left without saying the Prayer for the Dead.

Only once had Liza wanted a boy badly enough. She was thirteen, and in love with Brendan Dugan. She first noticed him at the warm-up house at Cedarbrook Pond where the eighth graders met for skating. Tall, slender, with brown hair almost black he combed across his forehead like a wing. When she looked at his angular face and high cheekbones, forming caves under blown almond eyes, she talked loudly to get his attention and pushed near him in the circle of skaters.

The boys formed a whip and sped over the ice, grabbing giggling girls who then screamed as the whip snapped at the end and they careened into the soft snow. She stayed apart until they tired and broke into pairs. Then she skated over to Brendan Dugan and stood next to him, calling out to Monica Smith, who lay spent on the ice. They skated, and she pretended not to see her friends, following with furtive smiles. Later, inside the warm-up house, she took off her skates and sat near him on the bench to rest her feet on the pot-bellied stove.

Soon everyone knew she was Brendan Dugan's girl. Her father gave grudging permission for her to go to a public school dance. The lawn in front of Central School moved with teenagers, and smoke coated budding branches in the woods. Brendan dropped his arm over her shoulder. Inside, the band set up, and couples necked on piles of coats. Brendan flattened his body next to hers in the first slow dance; she copied the way the other girls swung their hips.

By the end of the dance, her ribs ached from the pressure of his body. She waited as the final song began, his face in her hair, ready for the kiss. When it came, his lips firm, she moved against him. Then he pushed his tongue against her teeth, his arm hard on her back. Slowly she parted, feeling the tip of his tongue enter her mouth. A moment more and she pulled back, scraping his tongue. He nursed it.

"Why did you pull away?"

"I didn't like what you were doing."

"Haven't you ever. . ."

"No."

Neither of them spoke on the way home. Under the streetlights his black hair shone. She liked the fine bones of his face and wanted to touch the caves under his cheekbones. A few houses from hers she stopped and backed into the hedge.

"What's wrong?"

She pulled his jacket. "Please kiss me again."

He hesitated. "Please."

Their tongues played and she let him kiss her neck and throat. Then she backed away, holding his hand.

"You liked it that time."

"Yes, but I don't want to go any further."

"Why?"

"It's wrong."

"Who says?"

"Father Murphy and the nuns."

"They'll always tell you the best things are wrong."

"It's sinful."

"What is?"

"Necking."

"We just necked, Liza."

"We didn't."

"Sure we did. Now, when I kissed you. Was that a sin?"

"I better go home."

When Brenda Dugan hadn't phoned in two weeks, she knew he'd dropped her for another girl. At night she waited for the house to hush and then pressed her forehead against the cold glass to look at the magnolia blossoms gleaming from the lawn below. The pigeons brooded on Fisher's roof and dropped white on the pink petals. Under the tree Brendan lay with his face in blonde hair and his hands cupping large cotton breasts. They shook loose the sticky flowers and she heard murmers from a row of pale faces that watched from the fence. She knew they saw her through the third-floor window with no blinds only curtains that hid nothing. The girl's lips followed the curve of his cheeks into the soft caves. Then they were gone and only the white clusters remained on the trees.

Norita Dittberner Larson

PHOTOGRAPH IN YESTERDAY'S PAPER

Seven years into your stroke,
I cross your silence the way I enter Monday morning
or flip through yesterday's paper
not seeing
until I notice an African woman
standing with her staff
in the middle of my kitchen

her face almost
breaks   she is caught in the moment
when birds suck in breath
the lines of her mouth strained
from not singing

and you behind her
as I have seen you a hundred times
the floodwaters rising in you
pressing for shape at your lips   words
that never arrive   that dart
in your hands
like lost fish

mother
I keep dipping that morning
in my words
and never come close to the moment
you and the African
sat in my kitchen
awaiting the gift of tongues

WHAT GROWS WILD

Here, among the sweet-faced daffodils
stands the rhubarb,
spreading its rumors of flesh,
stalks whistling songs you never learned
in school,
making you remember a time
long ago or last week
when you held the core of night
in your hand.

It was July all summer,
nights of heat pressing the walls
of my parents' house,
you agreeing with everything
my father said,
about the freedom riders
about the war
about fishing.
We watched him doze,
the newsflash said "Man sleeps
during the ten o'clock news, can't last
much longer."
When the house was quiet with breathing
we left it for the tall grass
behind the clothesline
where our bodies opened
and sang with longing.

Chop it, dice it,
sweeten it with sugar,
make bread, cakes, pies
roll them and roll them
as fast as you can,
rhubarb will be back
uncurling like a fist
into blossom,
stubborn as the body
which will not forget
the wilderness it knows.

TUESDAY

My arms ache.
The day is a mule, I'm dragging
the rope over my shoulder.
Noontime passes,
sundown.

I am peeling potatoes
when you come home, stepping over
the shoes, coats,
the children's schoolbooks forgotten
in their hunger.

After supper
we talk about the foods our mothers cooked.
I didn't know
we had potatoes in common,
boiled and flaking
in a bowl of cracked china.

Outside the wind crosses the yard
and shakes the back of the house.
You undress
and looking at your nude body
I say "You know, we look funny
without fur."
"Yes," you answer,
"kind of plain."

Most nights we don't leap into bed
but come to it grateful
for a body that keeps on warming
for the imprint of flesh
real as potatoes
and the beast asleep at the door.

A DEATH, ON YOUR MOTHER'S SIDE

We head West in the pick-up, leave behind
our children.
The box between us holds our good clothes,
newspapers,
a map marked in red.

Into South Dakota on a wide curve
you remember your mother,
how she drove into pheasants,
the blood-splattered feathers on the windshield,
Frances of the dark eyes,
of weekend trips back home,
your uncle's saloon, the revel
on Sundays while the roast beef burned
and you played blackjack
in the corner.

We enter the town like the ghost
of a parade. Ahead of us
the wind uproots a sagebrush and drives it
down a row of shops flat-faced
against the curb. There is no one
to ask directions.

We find your uncle in an unmarked house
on Main Street,
a room of empty folding chairs.
He is small in his coffin,
he looks bad, you tell me, as if
something were still in the balance.

The family is gathered in a pocket
at the edge of town,
we sit in the yoke of the ceiling light, caught
in a day falling inward,
so much death, even the house
is for sale.

I ask you with my eyes
why
we came.

Then familiar hands touch us.
In the kitchen the counters are lined
with fluted cakes,
sausages and ham.
Your cousin offers us whiskey.
Oh the stories
we tell.

FAMILY REUNION   1950

when you whisper
they don't stoop
down

uncles are more like trees
you cross the grass
climb up

ACROSS THE DRIVEWAY

For weeks you don't see her
then one night
on the way to empty the garbage
you tell her everything.

She sends over the clothes
her children outgrow,
never entertains the same night you do
knowing you both
will need the ice bucket,
knows the state of your closets
but won't tell.

And when the trouble at her house
stops at the windowsill,
when some private grief overturns
the lawnchairs
you can wait.
Rituals of necessity connect you—
sooner or later
one of you will need eggs.

CONVERSATIONS AT THE END OF MARCH

On the boulevard
a patch of snow pulls away from the curb
drawing
to a final density

By late April
you won't notice what's left
a black tooth
rudimentary
and useless

Cranberries have the same habit
they dangle from their stems far into December
empty
except for their color
against the snow

Between seasons we remember
the remnants left
in the drawer
photographs
bookmarks
all smelling of absence and leather

Yesterday when you opened it
each artifact testified
you listened
as if swimming in your first waters
you discovered gills
and almost turned back

WEST SEVENTH STREET

Essence of beer pours
from the smokestacks at the brewery

This section of the city is dedicated to repairs
rebuilt transmissions
used appliances.
At every corner its lineage is tacked:
Old Fort Road begat
West Seventh   the hooves of cattle beat
this ground   this street still
has the heart muscle
of an ox

The bus-driver knows it, see
how he leans back
turns the wheel with one finger?
This is his run   more
than the skyways downtown unbuttressed
by dirt

He learned the blunt edge of the knife here
the language of plumbers
who name their parts male and female
because one fits into
the other

Today he watches for Spring four times
twice uptown
twice downtown.
It squints off the bits of glass, rises
in a breeze off the river

The river so close
he forgets
living here
that before the oxen
was the river
flicking its tongue at the land

Carl Lindner

MISMATCH

The courts wait, wide open.
Children fool, dreaming airily of shots.
Heavy men puff, out of step,
laboring to regain
what dribbles out of bounds.

Today I overslept and found
the sides chosen with a place
for me. Match-ups disclosed
how far short my team must fall.
Play or decline?
I played.
       I lunged for something gone,
a ball that spun away, bodies
slipping through my arms like smoke,
before I'd thought to move.
They wove a net that tangled us
where we stood, as they danced
and floated up to the rim.
Yet, once before, it happened:
secure in their heightened grace,
unaware, they sparked and fanned a flame
that burned clear down to my sneakered soles
and we got ahead, somehow, and stayed
there, hanging on until the end.

A WEREWOLF'S LIFE

A werewolf's life is never easy.
Yellow moon-face, gleaming as a tusk,
you rouse me again, begin a hum
beneath a coat of fur.
My tongue curls a molar.
Doppelganger darling,
I will tear your heart, snarling
my joy, blind for the moment to risk—
I who have tiptoed the cozy
dark, never at ease in a bedroom
world. The weaker wolf bares its breast
and belly to signal surrender;
the stronger walks away. No way, dearest,
my heart is a red marauder.

FIRST FROST

In mid-October morning light
the earth wears a grizzle.
Upright blades
are stiff as three-day stubble,
white with a tinge of blue.
Today the sun—
a disc
of platinum on fire—
will reclaim the green,
hold it a little longer
against the coming season.
I feel again the five-o'clock
shadow on my father's cheek.

TAKING ONESELF IN HAND

Hello body, saddlebag,
worn leather stitched and creased
on yet another trail.
What lies in wait?

You still own the shakes
when the dark drapes your bunk
and a dangling man of a robe
collared by a nail
starts to move.

Between your bowing legs
swings a wrinkled sack
where nuggets jounce like stones
as you shop the gullies and ravines.
Together they strike, generate
a stream of golden particles,
ore that runs in a hidden vein.

So pack your ass, old desert rat,
hunt for the mine's mouth
all you will;
scrape your horny hands,
your bony knees on pebble and shale.

But scan, above all,
this cracked and bouldered land
for that desperado whose ambush never fails,
whose features notch no wanted poster,
shifty-faced as desert sand.

Perhaps the time has come
to turn from this prospector's life,
to fold away my dusty clothes,
to hunker down,
complacent as a grinning skull
boxed in a canyon.

Thirty-five, I'm halfway there
to camp my bones beside a dying fire,
please myself with a baked potato,
trace for a partner's graying ear
my bowels' history.
Not yet, not yet—
no unbroken stallion
lightly wears a bridle or corral.
Here is a friend to stand with me,
ready to hand as a balanced gun,
snug yet loose in its holster.

CARDINAL: A LOVE POEM

Blood on the wing,
a tongue of fire,
down you come
to earth to light
a thatch of green.
Always before
I have watched you fly
into blue, sometimes burning through
the white corpse of winter,
but always away from me.
Until today.
Scarlet kiss—
a flutter
and a pulse away
you light.

VAMPIRE

If you find me
sleeping in my box,
there are things
you can try:

you may lop off my head,
but then you must keep it
forever from my body

you may drive a stake
of aspen (from the cross)
of whitethorn (from the crown)
through my navel;
this transfixes me
if done
with a single blow—
a second try
and I catch your hand

you may drop a crucifix
or sprinkle holy water
on my skin,
then watch me
sizzle and curl
as I turn my lungs
inside out for you

all things considered,
burning is best;
all that remains
you carry
to a windy height
and let the air
lick me clean.

If you fail
I'll home in
on your heartbeat,

nuzzle your neck awhile
before I pierce your skin.
As I drink your body's wine
both of us will drown,
but one of us
at least will rise again.

A FIRE AT NIGHT

I love the dancing light
the blue becoming
orange, blood-red
fingertips
probing the black
I dream it will burn
forever like a heart

I draw myself
close, warming my hands
calculating how
long it will last
checking around
for wood, patting
my pocket for matches

I wonder at licking
flames, tongues I speak,
savage with my eyes
my belly that pit
dropping down and down
I want it all
and I want it now

a fire at night
and me, burning

WATER

Ninety-six percent
of me is you,
but when I am in you
I go under.
True,
you do your best
to buoy me up.
I like your trying
to teach a stone
something
other than down.

Running under the sun
squeezes you
out of me.
In a fountain
you wait to spring,
soft, silver curve
summoning the lips,
and I bend for you.
I can't get enough.
You are like first love.

And you're at home
everywhere.
Skydiver,
from clouds you drop
down to earth
without wings
parachute
or safety net.
Unlike a heart
you need nothing
to break your fall.

There is no keeping
you down.
Buried,

you rise again.
Christians
like to think a man
once walked on you.

How you circulate,
always coming back
in your own sweet time.
Light-
bender, shimmer-flow.

PURSUING LIGHT

ever since
the opening, the glare
you follow light

seeing it break
into color, nuance
in prisms
of glass and water

watching it bounce
off the silver
of a looking glass
or leap from puddle
pool or cresting wave

so what if it deceives—
images being
real or virtual
the living eye
reflects
and drinks the light

so long as it ripples
in heat-shimmer
over asphalt
counterfeiting wet spots
the ripple of a hand
that waves goodby
as you approach
you cannot look away

and there is no holding it

AFTER A DISCONNECT

The operator's voice, gray,
goes with a permanent,
goes with her grudging-
ly accepting her husband's
late-night calls when
they're too urgent to be
put on hold again.

She's got my number
now. I blush,
a man going thin
on top, thick in the middle,
spanked and sent to my room.

Make a game
hide your shame
never tell
your real name.

The dream comes back—
cut off, no
air that vibrates, flows
up the windpipe,

larynx a voice-box,
dead,
my ears muffled in dirt,
twin receivers
off the hook.

The old death-dream—
no one to call.
Coffined, cribbed
in a little cell.
A telephone booth
is a private hell.

A forefinger on
each temple, I call
my blood. Babies
we must make do,
make do.

Catherine Stearns

THE HANGING HORSE

whose two ears were delicate
and as unlikely to twitch
as pointed ferns etched
in glass; whose dark coat gleamed
with the colorless fluid
of some ghostly libation;
whose decorous head first
sniffed at the strange fear
rising off a pier on the St. Lawrence river.
Up near the tip
of an old arm, rigid
in the sling of two webbed bands,
his tail blown back straight in the wind,
my horse became a giant
wheather vane.
And I knew then
the freight of my feeling
—dipping, dipping
with each frantic hoof
beneath his slick shoulders—
and how quickly strands of fog
loop out across the river
into a night that grows older,
into a mind that grows colder.

HONEYMOONING AT THE PAMODZI

(The Pamodzi is an elegant hotel in Lusaka, Zambia. The speaker is a
member of the Tonga tribe in Kafue, not far from Lusaka. *Muka Joni*
means John's wife.)

I keep one eye open
to see what my husband does—
under these silk sheets
he looks like a white man.
This bed's big enough
for me and all my sisters
who are not yet married;
I am *Muka Joni, Muka Joni.*
Last night, I admit
I was a little girl
when he asked me to brush
my body with powder,
for the smell of dust
provokes the ghosts in my head.
Not that I won't adorn myself!
On my wedding day I tied
rattles and bells on my legs
when we danced in the daylight
where everyone could see
the tattoos on my chest
like palm fruits, the tattoos
on my back like stars.

This morning I missed
the roosters crowing,
my sisters, shaking their gourds.
But I am *Muka Joni.*
When I turn on a game show,
women like me
win pots and copper plates.
I think: I can be on TV
now I'm a rich man's wife.
Because I know
how to use the red ochre,
my bride-prince was ten cattle.

At the Pamodzi there is water,
cold water and hot water,
but the roof is flat and low.
The roof of my mother's house
was laced with elephant grass.
I remember when death came
to fetch my brother
without even brushing the dust
off his buttocks, my mother
tried to hold him higher
than death could reach.
But when he comes—
in spite of rhinoceros horn,
crucifixes, dancing—
you cannot resist.

My husband's lips are dry,
but not as cracked as earth
in the dry season.
He doesn't wake as I kiss him.
Downstairs, breakfast is
coffee and eggs and meat.
I won't have the meat myself,
but I think my husband will.
In the elevators are mirrors
to see how lucky I am.
Muka Joni, Muka Joni.
When I go to the swimming pool,
surrounded by a high wall,
I swim up and down, hard
past the sirens in the street
and the girls I know there
begging, past their children
who move like poisoned fish,
and past the ghost of my brother.
When I have finished,
I call for the towel-giver
(he looks like my cousin, Chamuka)
who forgets himself and hisses
at me like a wounded snake.
How I could laugh

in his unlucky face
when my new husband,
worth ten of him,
dresses upstairs in the military
and wears darkglasses
to shield his eyes
from the flies.

SONNET TO SPONTANEITY

At times your life seems to have nothing
to do with you. You peel the vegetables,
fill the days with clutter of dishes, strangers,
perhaps a lover. You find ways to live,
finish dinner, go to bed. But you are not
there, not yet.
You are remembering
the tall yellow house where you lived once
in the window, watching the men dig up
the garden. Nothing was supposed to be there,
nothing but the graves of small animals,
what you thought of as *things with no insides*.
Still, you expected something, someone
crouching in the hole.

HAIR WHICH CAN BE MAGIC DISAPPEARS

On the same day the eldest Ashanti daughter
has her head shaved—
an act of mourning
her chief and father—

another woman in a different country
is grabbed by the hair
from behind. Her first
bruises, like the royal-

blue of the cerements in Ghana, map
yet another country
from which the will
has been banished.

*

I used to let my hair fly like a child's
passion, although I feared
that one day I'd be riding
my red horse

and catch it, like Absalom, on a tree.
I learned to like the scissors'
shock of repeated sound,
and how I felt

invulnerably lighter as hair fell down my back.
Sometimes I saw my father
hiding behind my mother's
dark hair-tent

that skirted over their wrists as they danced.
And when she cut it, I saw
the long line of her jaw
not unlike my own.

*

In this city, there are women tattooed
with words: when they fling
the hair away from their
mouths, their breasts,

poems—connected by the body—appear.

NOTHING

If I understood, then what could you say?

Counting the months as the Chinese do
in which you were part of another,
you are almost through with life.

As I think of you, the man
at my table swallows.
It was not nothing

to care for you.

A GERMAN WOMAN, 1946

Either it's fun or it isn't
my man said to me after we married.
In the woods, out walking,
he addressed the trees:
I'll chop down the lot of you!
He was a carpenter but unemployed,
and we lived with his parents
in a little room.
If you get big girl you'll have to go,
his mother said to me one day;
then his father said war.
There was no child. For slaughter
I wouldn't have one, although a daughter
could have kept me company
in the lonely room.
After the penal-battalion,
and prisoners-of-war coming home,
a soldier drinking said:
you're as dead as this country.
So I exchanged the wooden cradle
for ribbons and trinkets.
A bad deal you made, I tell myself,
giving it all to a dirty medal.
And when I see a couple against a pine,
I know it's not over.
She's young and slips her cold
hand underneath his sweater.

ADVICE FROM AN UNKNOWN WOMAN

This is not the only place to live,
but when I go away,
I'm at the end of a string.

I used to strut my stuff
when the landlord came. I've waited long
for this touch of beauty, this class.

Lately my bones have responded
to a warmth. It's all around us.
Don't you feel it in the air?

There's something different going on,
something famous. I pick up its presence
on my radar. All my life I've tried

to send signals across the mud.
I look out now and see life
ripe and green. Who planted it?

Where did it come from? Take the old
lightbulb out and burn everything yellow.
We'll have a carnival tomorrow.

Nancy Rotenberry

TO THANK R. K. FOR THE PHOTO OF LAKE MILLE LACS

You called the fall day ominous;
       it was blue-gray, at the edge
of winter, yes. I remember summer
       packed her steamer trunk one
August night full of yellow birch
leaves. That was all we saw of her.

    When I looked again, white lace
branches waited to be wedded to a
       winter sky, ready for a union
under sheets of snow. And the fringe
of brown rye grass, loving to be green,
       solemn as a prayer rug,
knelt imploring at waterside.

THE LAST SEASON

We cut two limbs from the old apple tree—
wormy, rotting fruit tumbled to the ground.
It gave richly until this malady.
We cut two limbs from the old apple tree.
Birds were housed and squirrels fed liberally
each season, while it was healthy and sound.
We cut two limbs from the old apple tree—
wormy, rotting fruit tumbled to the ground.

FOR MAIZIE THE CAT

No life in the drab backyard
until a young cat appears,
padding around the sidewalk's bend
on its way home.
And life stirs:
a cardinal flies to the purple plum,
     carving scarlet on the snow;
a black-capped chickadee flutters in
to the tree's other half;
six more light in the nearer birch:
     all drawn by the menace,
     the predatory *felinus*
     domesticus,
     all squawking continuous
     ruckus
like jealous wives threatened by
another,
     who pads on . . .
too well-fed to care.

DRY SEPTEMBER

Riverbank weeds are dying
    Indian's tobacco
        Cocklebur and thistle
            Parted lips of milkweed pods
               You can hear the weeds
                  Listen this cool September
              Browning in the breeze
           Spilling seedpearl teeth
        Swaying spiky crowns
     Curing crumbly brown
Drying in the breeze.

MARTIN'S

been puffing on a cigar for sixty years,
molars and lips clamping it in place, or
getting ready to light up by slipping off the
crunchy cellophane, nipping off the bitter tip
with his front teeth, scuttling wrapper and end

but first remembering to remove, untorn, phlegmatic
Dutchmen, sensuous shawl-draped Muriels, gold and
ruby cigarband rings sealing my earliest amours.
He puffed fragrant wooden boxes into
dollbeds and wardrobes, whole apartment complexes,

hopscotch chalk or crayon box, treasure chest for
Crackerjack whistles and Captain Midnight secret
decoders . . . he probably puffed leaning over my cradle,
curly black hair, Errol Flynn handsome; everyone
accepted the black-ringed holes dotting shirtfronts

scorched by descending sparks, and at the end of
dinner focused on the lengthening ash, not the
conversation. He puffed upstairs to kiss goodnight,
stopping long enough to puff out the light and like a
magician's string of scarves could endlessly multiply

cigars, flipping off a second from the first in his
fingers, pocketing it to produce another and another
without ever filling the pocket. Often he was puffing
on Sunday mornings when I climbed on the arm of his soft
green chair to see Joe Palooka, Maggie and Jiggs, the

Katzenjammer Kids all enveloped in a hypnotic haze. I
know he puffed on a birthday feverish with chickenpox or
mumps, yellow warning posted for the world at large;
in the August dusk his drowsy tale punctuated
by an on-off glow comforting as a lighthouse beacon
on a stormy night.

For my father

WITH CHISELED NAME AND BIRTH DATE ONLY

Our bodies heavy with chicken and cake
from the churchyard picnic, the Ford
struggling up the hill through the gate,
we watched the older faces
for what we should feel in this place,
they searching ahead for the family
plot lying beneath a tamarack tree.

We brought honeyed lilacs
kept fresh from town in weighted mason
jars, and geraniums to plant
blood red against the polished granite.
Blown by wind from the cornfields we ran
among the stones, bending back grass
covering names of our kin.

And even then we noticed that off to the
south where the corn rows grow
there's a lot more room in Chester Hill.

FOR ONE GROWING OLD

For my mother

I am memorizing the leaves
still holding in November's breath
the way I memorize your face.
Seeing first your platinum hair
I am memorizing the leaves
before they drop into the streets.

FRANKLIN AVENUE BRIDGE

I

DAVE LOVES DIANE ALWAYS painted on the bridge
    arching the road like a rainbow.
    He loves her. He loves her always.
    The pot of gold is now, says Dave,
    AND at the end. The colors he vows
    won't fade in the wash. They'll
    always be bright as those leaves
    dropping down. Bright as the trees
    lining the banks.

II

    But Dave, I'm embarrassed.
    This road should be closed to the public.
    Your message is one to be whispered
    together in close day or close night.
    And I picture you painting upside-down
    to shout as Diane drives under.

III

    Yes, Dave, I'm doubly embarrassed.
    This road should decidedly close.
    For while you   lovesick   hang upside-down
    the leaves are turning brown.

FECUND NIGHT

                    heavy   warm
alive with mating
flashing light.

Promising ecstasy
frogs and cicadas trill
enticement
into the clouded black

where thunder drums
on the lake and woods
lightning
crowns the horizon.

Skimming grass and bushes
fireflies
blazing torches pulsing
find each other
and mate.

And inside the cabin
wet grass
still clinging to our
feet
alive with mating
we couple.

WAITING TIMES

When she woke before her parents
in the north summer cabin,
eased the screen door shut,
went quiet into the resinous world
waiting for a pine to drop a cone,
pungent, sticky,
into her stretching hands.

Or squatted with gulls,
hungering breakfast,
on forbidden black basalt
slabbed against Superior's shoreline
waiting for fish,
blooming gold in morning-fresh sun,
to leap from water into beak.

Or stood on a station platform
waiting for a train,
long ceased running,
to an Iowa town
buried in cornstalks and clover.

Or hunkered on chipped cement
on Grandma's front steps
on the Fourth of July
waiting for slow country darkness
to propel sparklers over bush and grass
in arm's length figure eights.

And on windy summer nights
there was waiting
sitting on wild cabbage leaves
in a vacant lot,
hearing distant thunder,
seeing dark stars move.
Waiting for life.

She did not know it had begun.

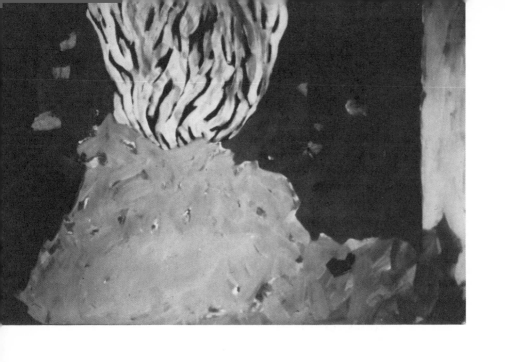

Jane O'Connell Nowak

AN ORPHAN IN THE FAMILY

I

By my fifteenth birthday, I was 5 feet 5 inches and weighed 175 pounds. That night, after I had eaten half of my birthday cake, my mother looked at me with obvious disgust.

"Frank," she said to my father, "take a look at your daughter."

"She looks good to me," he said, hiding behind his newspaper, not even looking up.

"Leave some cake for someone else," she snapped at me. "It may be your birthday, but you don't have to behave like a pig. Pretty soon, you'll look like the side of a barn. Frank, I insist that you look at your daughter."

He looked nervously at my mother, not at me.

"We have to do something with her," my mother said. "I can't stand the thought of her sitting around all summer, whining, stuffing herself and reading."

"She get good marks," said my brave champion.

"Who cares what kind of marks she gets? She'll never get a husband with that body and that disposition. Sulky! Fresh! Gloomy! She has no friends!"

"It will work itself out," he stammered.

"God helps those who help themselves," she answered with her usual originality. "She'll have to go to camp this summer. That's the only way. Fresh air and a regular bedtime might help her terrible personality and exercise will get some weight off her."

"I can't afford to send her to camp," my father said.

"So what else is new?" my mother answered.

"I won't go," I shrieked. I wasn't going to get undressed in front of a group of girls, every one of whom would be slimmer and prettier than I.

"You will go," my mother insisted. I could tell that she meant it. "I've saved five hundred dollars out of the house-hold money. All we have to do is scrape together another five hundred and we'll be able to send you." She turned to my father. "If you get together that second five hundred, you'll get some of it back. After all, I'll save a lot of money on food with her away."

Thanks a lot, I thought. Who keeps filling my plate?

But part of me did want to go—it would be a change. And there was absolutely nothing to do in the summers in Watertown, except babysit, but that usually depressed me a lot. I hated to see those pretty, thin wives all dressed up, going out to have dinner with their husbands. I always felt like Cinderella when they left, home by the hearth, usually with a wet, screaming kid to look after. Besides, these people never had good things to eat. Bean sprouts and granola bars did not qualify as babysitting munchies in my book.

Things wouldn't have been too bad either if I had a license and a car. Needless to say, I had neither. The only way I could get to swim was a long bus ride, and going anywhere by bus was usually a major undertaking. So it was a choice of staying home in the heat, babysitting, riding the bus or going to camp.

Nevertheless, I didn't really expect things to be any better at camp than they were at home. At fifteen, I was a confirmed pessimist.

We went to Filene's on Winter Street in Boston for camp clothes. "Fortunately, they wear uniforms," my mother said, "so it won't matter if you don't have many clothes."

And with that misconception, I was supposedly set for camp.

II

My mother knew as little about camp clothes as she knew about everything else. In fact, I have never known anyone to have so many opinions about things she knew nothing about. Sure the brochure said, "uniforms," but as soon as we got to the Camp and I saw all the other girls in their designer jeans and cashmere sweaters, I knew I had made a mistake.

There were six other fifteen year olds in the bunk house, plus Betsy Chandler, the counselor, whose major counseling activities consisted of tweezing her eyebrows and squeezing her pimples. Betsy languidly explained to me that everyone was assigned a cot and a row of four open cubicles. That's all she said. The other girls had all known one another since they were ten. They were flitting all over the place in various states of dress, squealing and laughing hysterically at the mention of boys' names. A stereo blasted.

The cubicles and bed next to mine belonged to Andrea, known to her friends as Andy. My throat and heart ached when she turned to me and smiled. Why couldn't I have been born Andy? My mother always sarcastically said that I would sell my soul for candy. She was wrong. I'd sell my soul for good looks, golden looks, slim legs, curly hair, smooth white skin, and brown eyes. It was so unfair to be born like me.

"Hi," Andy said. She had a perfect post-braces smile. "Are you finished unpacking?"

I nodded.

"Well, if you're going to use only one cubicle, can I use your others?" She flashed that smile again. "I'm going out of my mind with clothes. My mother's a buying fool. God only knows what she'll send me this summer from Ireland. You know how mothers are. So, can I have the rest of your shelves?" She started moving those wonderful clothes onto my empty shelves.

"No," I said.

She looked at me politely. Puzzled, but polite. "I beg your pardon," she said. There was only a tiny smile now.

"No," I repeated. "They're my cubicles. I need them." I looked down at my sneakers.

"But you've emptied your trunk," she said, trying to appeal to my sense of reason and fair play. How irrational of me to deny her what she wanted.

We had now become theater. The other girls stopped their activities and watched.

"My mother is going to send me more clothes too," I said.

"I'll give the cubicles back to you when your clothes come," she said. Still calm, still self-possessed, still certain that when I saw the error of my reasoning I would grant her anything.

"Until then," I said, "I'm going to use them for my books. My library lets you take out twenty books during the summer." I pointed to the stack of books under my cot. "I was just about to put them on my shelves."

"My dear girl," she said, "books are perfectly safe on the floor. Clothes are not."

"No," I repeated, "they're my cubicles, and I have to take very good care of these books."

"Oh, for heaven's sake," Andy said with a bit of heat, "if anything happens to your books, I'll give you a few bucks to pay for them. Now can I have the cubicles?"

I knew I was courting trouble. But I couldn't stand the contrast between us. Her cot had become a luxurious station in the center of the bunk house— embellished by a little throw rug, multicolored cushions, a portable stereo, a radio, and bottles of Chanel #5 and Charlie cologne. I hated her for having everything I wanted and for being everything I wasn't and never would be.

"No," I repeated sullenly, "you can't have the cubicles."

"But, why?" she almost wailed. She really didn't know what it was to be frustrated, to have someone say no and no and no to that pretty face.

"Because they're mine," I said. I turned my back on her and started to read.

Andy rolled her eyes at her audience, shrugged her shoulders, and won in losing. My summer at Camp Mickmack was determined at that moment.

In many ways camp was an extension of school. Up at dawn to the sound of a recorded bugle, shiver during flag raising, eat breakfast, clean up, swim, eat lunch, rest, pursue an afternoon activity, go to bed to the sound of taps (recorded)—and then the whole routine began the next day again. There was no deviation. It was "everybody up," "everybody out," and "everybody in."

Most of the summer was merely a rehearsal for the Color War of the last two weeks of camp. Everybody got all emotional about Color War. I thought it was a dumb idea, but I didn't dare say so. What difference did it make if green or yellow won? All I wanted to do was lie on my cot and read. But the girls with the exact opposite attitudes won the Good Camper awards.

Another thing I didn't like was that life at Camp Mickmack was led in double lines. Everything was a march two-by-two—to meals, to movies, to campfires, on bus trips, on duty details. The only place you went without a partner was the bathroom. But I was always the odd one, the one without a partner. Counselor Betsy was forced to sit with me whenever we went anywhere. Each time it happened she'd mutter, "I guess we're partners again."

Betsy was an old camper who had graduated to counselor. She acted as if she owned the camp. I noticed a strange thing about Betsy. She wasn't pretty—she looked a little like a weasel—but there seemed to be some kind of conspiracy to make her think she was pretty. Girls would say things like, "Don't you just adore pointy chins?" or "Isn't Betsy the most intelligent-looking girl you ever saw?" Maybe old campers just take care of their own.

I was an undesirable outsider to Betsy. About the only thing that would have helped me, after she noted my lack of friends, clothes, and possessions, would have been if I had flattered her. I could have said something like, "I think it's the cutest thing for people to look like rats." But I didn't say anything.

Betsy was part of the camp system, and the camp system was the same system I had come to understand from life. If you weren't popular or pretty or well-built, only money could help you. And I had nothing to help me.

Each mail call advertised my family's lack of money. The twice-a-week delivery would bring packages of delights for the girls, and their parents often included gifts for Betsy—something from Canada, from San Francisco, from the Caribbean. Betsy's dresser top started to look like a souvenier store.

My parents never sent packages of clothing or food. They assumed that the camp fee covered all "extras." I charged a few toiletries at the camp canteen and tried not to think about the scene at the end of the summer when my parents received the bill. I was always worrying about things like that, guilty about money, never carefree like the other girls.

Their food packages arrived with indulgent notes: "Share with the others." "Let me know when you need more." "Enjoy yourselves, little piggies."

The foods they received fascinated me, and I had to sit on my hands to restrain from pouncing. S.S. Pierce chocolates and butter crunch, jars of sour pickles and maraschino cherries, canned hams, boxes of dried apricots and cashew nuts and endless packages of sunflower seeds and pistachio nuts. Sometimes one package cost more than my mother spent on food for our family for a week.

After enough food had accumulated, the girls would have a massive picnic late at night, and sit around and talk and giggle. I would listen in wonder as they spoke about cutting school to go shopping at Bonwit's or Charles Sumner's. What joy to be so free! I never went anywhere at all. With school nuns and my mother ready to kill me if I even breathed the wrong way, such escapades really never seriously entered my mind. Besides, I never had any money, and anyway, what was the point of cutting alone?

During these pig-outs, I would sit on my cot pretending to read, hungrily watching them and the food. Eventually someone would call, "Come on, Fatso . . . come and get it." They didn't care that I couldn't reciprocate. I have to admit that they were generous. But it wasn't the kind of generosity where you're nice to a person because you care about that person. It was the generosity of indifference. They had so much that giving some of it away was a meaningless gesture.

Still, all in all, camp was better than my hot home in the city. After my first few days, I had established my loner routine, and it was almost without pain. But my peace didn't last long.

One night, it was my turn for dining room clean-up duty. I did it quickly and quietly, wiping off wooden tables, stacking glasses and silverware, sweeping my half of the dining hall. I had been reading "The Lord of the Flies," and I could hardly wait to get back to my bunk to finish it. But when I left the dining hall the moon was out and the scent of the pines stopped me from hurrying. I walked slowly, smelled the pines, looked at the moon, and felt pretty good for a change.

I opened the screen door to my bunk house, looked inside and saw a tableau. Betsy sat on Andy's bed, with her arm around her. Next to Andy sat Pat, a weak little toady. The others sat on the floor, in a straight row, a jury, waiting. Thinking this had nothing to do with me I walked toward my cot.

"Now, don't think you can escape by reading," Betsy's voice jolted me, as I reached for my book.

"Escape what?" I asked.

"You know damn well."

I shrugged and opened my book. Betsy walked over, grabbed it and threw it on the floor. My library book was ruined, the binding broken. I picked it up and hugged it to my chest.

Betsy's witch-like finger pointed to an empty food carton perched at the end of Andy's bed, "Don't tell me you don't know anything about this," she said.

"Well, I don't," I said. "I don't what you're talking about!" Why did my voice sound so guilty?

"It wasn't empty this afternoon," Betsy said. She sounded happy to hit back at me for the endless enforced partnerships.

"So why ask me?" I said.

"You were the only one here, reading as usual, while we were all out swimming."

Betsy's voice lashed me. The girls said nothing.

"I didn't touch anything," I quavered. "I certainly don't steal. And you're going to pay for this book."

"But you were the only one here," Pat whined. "And you don't get any packages from home. It's only logical."

"It may be logical," I said, "but it isn't true. Didn't you ever hear of circumstantial evidence? If any of you read mystery stories, you'd know that I'm the least likely person to have taken the food because of circumstantial evidence."

"Listen, smart ass," Betsy said, "this circumstantial evidence is right in front of us. I've been watching your greedy eyes devour those packages. The circumstantial evidence is that you stay fat and you never get packages from home. The food in the dining hall wouldn't make a mosquito fat, so you must have taken it."

"You've all just been looking for something to accuse me of." I was starting to cry.

"See," Pat said, "she's crying because she's guilty. That's a sure sign."

"We should never have permitted Mrs. Donahue to assign an outsider to our bunk house." Betsy sighed. "I knew from the very first that she wasn't our kind of girl."

I couldn't stop the tears. Whose kind of girl was I? "I didn't do it," I sobbed.

"Pat," Betsy said, "go for Mrs. Donahue. We're going to move Katie out of this bunk house. She can steal food from some other place."

I dashed into the bathroom, locked the door and took the little bottle of iodine from the first-aid kit. Could you really kill yourself with this?

"Katie," Betsy pounded on the door, "What are you doing in there?"

"I'm holding a bottle of iodine," I sobbed. "I'll drink it and kill myself because you're all so mean to me. Then you'll be sorry."

"You come out of there this minute," Betsy said. "You won't get away with this."

No point in answering.

I could hear them talking outside. Chattering voices. Scraps of what they were saying came through the door.

"Gee, this is the most exciting thing that ever happened at camp."

"Does she really mean it?"

"Maybe we'll get into trouble if she kills herself."

And then, clearly spoken this time. "You may get in trouble," Betsy said, "but I'll get fired. I'll kill her myself if she doesn't commit suicide."

And then some more chattering.

"Listen, if she kills herself, we'll have more cubicle space."

"The point is she was wrong for this bunk house right from the beginning. She doesn't use a deodorant or even shave her legs. And she's rotten at athletics. She spoils every team she's on."

"I've never seen a dead body before. Will she turn red if she drinks the iodine?"

"She's red already. With that stringy, blond hair and ruddy complexion, she looks like an Indian with a crummy dye job."

Wild, raucous laughter.

And then Betsy's voice again.

"You may think this is funny, but if I get canned, I'll have to go back to the heat of Boston. We have to try to get her out. Come on, all of you—cooperate."

"Yes," Andy said, "let's stop kidding around. We have to get her out for Betsy's sake."

Betsy's sake! Didn't anyone care about my sake?

"Katie, dear," Betsy's voice oozed through the door. "We want to help you. We want to be your friends. We'll give you all the food you want if only you'll come out."

Now I was not only a thief. Now they thought I could be bought. They didn't seem to know anything about pride. I really didn't want to die, but they couldn't buy me.

I sat on the toilet seat, brooding. They had everything—and they had each other, too. The only thing I could say for myself is that I never did mean things to other people. If only I could make them sorry.

I could visualize the headlines after I died. FIFTEEN YEAR OLD FAT GIRL COMMITS SUICIDE IN CAMP BUNKHOUSE. Or: UNJUSTLY ACCUSED UGLY GIRL LOSES DESIRE TO LIVE. Or: GIRL DIES IN BUNK HOUSE BATHROOM. FAREWELL NOTE BLAMES RATLIKE COUNSELOR.

I hadn't said anything for a long time. I could hear more excited whispering outside.

"We could put paper under the door and set it on fire," Pat suggested.

"Don't be stupid," Betsy snapped. "We'd burn down the bunk house."

"How will we go to the bathroom?" someone whined. "My orthodontist said I couldn't miss a single night's brushing."

"Go into the bunk house next door," Betsy snapped.

"But my toothbrush is in there, with her."

"You and your orthodontist will somehow survive."

Betsy pounded on the door again. "You little bitch," she hissed. "I knew you were a troublemaker the minute I saw you. If you think you're going to get me in trouble, you're greatly mistaken."

I studied my nails. I had managed to bite and bloody almost every cuticle. The other girls had long, pretty nails. Some of them had their own manicure sets and regularly went to the beauty salon for professional manicures. Even my mother couldn't afford to go to the beauty parlor.

My mother! Suddenly I remembered the sacrifice that had sent me to camp. There they were—my mother, father, sister, brother, and grandmother—all squeezed into that hot house in Watertown, all hoping I was having a good time. Instead, here I was, as usual messing things up, just the way I did at home. I started to cry again.

It was awful to be poor. My father had worked month after month, without a vacation, to send Phillip to college and me to camp. I could see my poor old grandmother, sitting hour after hour darning socks and patching clothes. And my mother, washing laundry in our basement and then carrying huge loads of it upstairs and out into the backyard, since we were too poor to own a clothes dryer. I thought of my weary, silent father, saving nickel by nickel the five hundred dollars he needed to send me here. I sat and wept at the injustice of things.

Then I heard heavy, no-nonsense footsteps outside the bathroom door. Mrs. Donahue! The girls tumbled over one another to tell her the story. Silence.

At last Mrs. Donahue said, "I confiscated the food while you were all at dinner. During my usual round of inspection, I saw a mouse scurry away from the box."

The girls all started to scream. "Stop that screaming, girls," Mrs. Donahue commanded. "Stop it at once, I say."

The screams stopped.

"Pick up the box, Andy," Mrs. Donahue said. "Now, open your eyes and look at things carefully, for a change. Do you see my note under the box? I put it there so that it wouldn't blow off your bed before you read it. I suggest you read it now."

Subdued, Andy read: "Food is not to be kept on floors. Food is not to be kept in cardboard boxes. All food that is not in metal boxes will be confiscated. I have taken the food from this box because there was mouse excrement in it. Mrs. Donahue."

"Yech," the girls moaned, "mouse excrement. My god, we're poisoned." Still no thought of me.

"Is this the first time you have heard me discuss this?"

"No, Mrs. Donahue."

"Is this the first time you've heard this, Betsy?"

"No, Mrs. Donahue." Betsy's voice was servile, humble, shaken.

"You, Betsy, are responsible for enforcing these rules. An old camper like you should certainly know the rules. Is that clear?"

"Yes, Mrs. Donahue."

"Now, does Katie have anything to do with this?"

"No, Mrs. Donahue."

"I expect that all of you, and you, Betsy, in particular, to see that this kind of incident does not happen again. Every girl in this bunk house pays exactly the same fee, and every girl is entitled to the same treatment. Is that clear?"

"Yes, Mrs. Donahue," Betsy muttered.

I was glad I had heard Mrs. Donahue say that. We were all paying the same fee—and it was much harder for my family to pay it. So why did I have to act and feel like a second class citizen? But I also understood that Betsy would never forgive me for losing the skirmish. She'd never stop trying to get even. I shivered.

Mrs. Donahue tapped briskly on the bathroom door. "Come out of there immediately, Katie." Her voice was firm, noncommittal, not angry, not warm. She usually resented any disturbance after she had retired to her own cabin, but her emotions were always in perfect control. Scared, I slid the bolt and opened the door. Nobody hugged me, touched me, smiled at me or said, "I'm sorry."

"Remember," Mrs. Donahue said to the group, "I cannot run a camp in which newcomers are not welcome. And I will not permit it. Lights out."

We all undressed silently and slipped into our beds. The others kept avoiding my eyes. That was all right with me. I felt so tired and depressed that I could hardly wait to get to sleep. But I lay awake for awhile thinking about what had happened. I knew that life wasn't supposed to be like this, but I didn't know how to make things different.

III

Uneasy truce! Nobody bothered me but nobody asked for my forgiveness or reached out to me. They tolerated me, avoided me, were indifferent to me. I never shared in the frantic squeals, secrets or whispers. I was either the last one chosen for the team or completely forgotten. Then I would escape quietly to the silent bunk house and my books. After the food incident, for the first time in my life, I was too unhappy to eat. Before I knew it, I had lost twenty-five pounds. I was beginning to like to look at myself in the mirror. This alone almost made camp worthwhile.

At the beginning of August, excitement ran through the camp. A dance had been scheduled for Saturday night with the boys' camp on the other side of Lake Mickmack. From our waterfront, we could see the boys across the lake, but we were not permitted to communicate with them. The middle of the lake was the invisible boundary.

All week the girls spoke of nothing but the dance. They spent Friday plucking, manicuring, snipping and deciding what to wear. I lay on my cot and read.

"I'm not going to the dance," I told Betsy.

"You have to go," she said.

"Why?"

"Because if you stay behind, a counselor has to stay with you."

"I don't need anyone," I said. "I can take care of myself."

"You have no choice," she said. "You have to go."

"What will you do?" I asked. "Drag me?"

"I suppose you're doing this to get back at me," Betsy said.

I looked at her silently, with contempt.

"I'll bet she doesn't want to go because she had nothing to wear," Pat said.

"Where are the clothes your mother was going to send you?" Andy asked sarcastically.

"I'm afraid if I go to Mrs. Donahue with this, she'll dock the entire bunk house," Betsy said. "She'll think we did something to poor Katie."

"I have an idea," Andy said. "Let's fix her up. You know, like when they take the glasses off a secretary and the boss suddenly realizes she's beautiful."

"No," I said. "Anyway, I don't wear glasses."

Andy ignored my response. I could see her getting excited by her idea. "Look," she said, "remember the play 'Pygmalion'? You remember—a rich man makes a lady out of a poor flower girl who can't speak good English and looks even worse than Katie."

"That's just a play," Pat said.

"But I think we can do it," Andy insisted.

"Will she let us?" asked another.

"Poor thing," said Pat.

They seemed to think that because I was fat, I was also deaf. They spoke about me as if I weren't there. But still I was intrigued. I think it was the words "poor thing" that got to me. That was the most sympathetic thing anyone had said about me all summer. Part of me wanted to see if the mysteries the girls learned from "Glamour Magazine" and their knowledgeable mothers would work for me.

"Good idea!" Betsy said. "It will be our bunk house project. I think this will get us back into Mrs. Donahue's good graces. We'll have to tweeze her eyebrows and squeeze her zits. It's a big job, but we can take turns if she'll sit still."

"Then we'll set her hair," said Andy. "She won't fit into any of our clothes, so we'll have to borrow a sweater and maybe a blouse from one of the other cabins. And, Betsy, you can lend her your pearl necklace."

"I'll lend her my deodorant."

"I'll lend her my Chanel #5."

"I'll lend her one of my hair ribbons."

Their eyes sparkled, their cheeks flushed. They were learning the pleasures of charity.

"We'll have to do something about her ruddy face color," Betsy said.

"I don't think we can," Andy answered. "I have some 'Cover Girl' make-up, but it's much too light for her. Maybe if we put lots of layers of foundation on her that will help."

"I don't want to go," I said, wanting them to convince me.

"Ungrateful!" Betsy snarled. "Why do you keep complicating things, trying to mess up this cabin? You're going. We'll make you look presentable—you'll see."

"Nobody will dance with me. Besides, I don't know how to dance."

"The room will be too crowded for any real dancing," Andy said. "You don't really have to know how, except when they play slow dances."

"But suppose nobody asks me?"

"We'll make them dance with you." Andy was fired with the vision of her idea. "I'll insist that any boy who wants to dance with me has to dance with you, too."

"It's not right to force anybody. I'd feel ashamed."

"Don't worry," Andy said. "They're only boys. You have to force them to do practically anything. But I want to tell you some things about when we get there. You'll have to stop biting your nails. Keep your hands out of your mouth. Hold up your head and smile. As soon as we get there, plaster a smile on your face and keep it there for the whole evening. Just keep smiling? All right?"

Degrading as it was, I couldn't help but find the experience exciting. At least people were taking some interest in me. Where else could I learn how to do these things? My mother never used make-up and we didn't get any magazines that girls read. Maybe they could accomplish a miracle. I would close my eyes and when they were through, I would look in the mirror and be thin and pretty.

The girls had begun the tweezing and squeezing and tears were running down my face.

"Tweezing hurts everyone the first time," Andy said. "But we have to take care of ourselves. Women who don't take care of themselves physically are society's rejects."

What about women who don't take care of themselves mentally? I asked myself. I didn't dare to say that aloud. My mother had always warned me that being a smart aleck was the surest way to offend people. Even if reading was my passion, it seemed that people did manage fine without it. Prettiness seemed to be more important than smartness.

Two hours later, eyebrows tweezed, pimples popped, make-up applied, hair curled, I studied myself in the mirror. No miracle. I still wasn't pretty, but at least I no longer looked like a subspecies. "Welcome to the human race," I dolefully murmured.

Andy sprayed my hair and throat with Chanel #5. What a lovely smell! My soul soared. All my mother used was Ivory soap. Ivory was all right, but it wasn't Chanel, a pretty girl's smell, a free, light, fresh smell. Someday I'd save up for a bottle of my own.

It was time to go. The girls surrounded me, pleased with their handiwork. But underneath, I was still myself.

I sat quietly on the bus, listening to their merry singing, feeling a hundred years older than they were. I wished with all my heart that I could be like them—unworried, happy. I dreaded the dance.

Too soon we reached the boys' camp. I saw the lights, heard the music from the stereo, and was so terrified that I sat rooted to the seat. Betsy saw me and thought I was backing down.

"Get up this minute," she snapped. "You are not going to stay on the bus. Just move. No trouble tonight, please. I want to have a good time, too. Now get up and march."

Praying for invisibility, I reluctantly walked off the bus. I did my fat-girl slink, hoping that nobody would notice me, as I followed Betsy into the noisy rec hall.

The hall rocked with music. Boys and girls reached out to one another. All about me couples were forming.

Loneliness in the midst of people is even worse than being alone. I sat there, feeling very awkward. After awhile, I got up self-consciously and slunk across the room, staying close to one wall, until I reached the refreshment table. I filled a plate, piling food on top of food. I even took food I hated, like potato salad.

Betsy was at one end of the table holding a cup of punch in her hand and talking with a handsome boy counselor. He looked like just the kind of boy who would be right for Nancy Drew. Betsy seemed to be scolding him, but he was laughing. Was it possible that she would treat this handsome man the way she treated me? He didn't seem to mind. He just laughed.

They stopped talking, looked over at me, then began to laugh and talk again. I thought that they might be laughing at me. Perhaps they were both disgusted with how much food I'd taken. He started to walk towards me and I almost bolted. He was probably going to tell me to put some food back so there would be enough left for the others. I put the plate down on the table and waited for the scolding. I looked at the floor.

"Hi," he said. He had a soft, southern voice, the first one I had ever heard in real life. "Betsy tells me you're new this year. Would you like to dance?"

I was paralyzed. Finally I muttered, still not daring to look at him. "Are you asking me to dance?"

"I sure am." He smiled.

"You want to dance with me?" I asked suspiciously. "Why?"

"Why?" he echoed. "I'll tell you why. Cause it's my party."

"Your party? Is it your birthday?"

"No." He laughed, head thrown back, warm smile, friendly, no malice.

"I'm the social director here, and everybody has to dance."

"Did Betsy ask you to dance with me?"

"Now, honey," he said, "what makes you think Betsy would do anything nice for another human being?"

I giggled, but I still wasn't ready to dance. "Was Betsy telling you something about me?"

He nodded.

"What was she saying?" I asked.

"What difference does it make what Betsy was saying?" he countered.

"I always have to know," I said, "even if it hurts me."

"Then you're just the opposite of me," he said seriously. "I want to hide from anything that could hurt me."

"Can people like you be hurt?" I asked. I didn't mean to say that. It just popped out. I was embarrassed at asking such a personal question.

"Shall we dance?" he asked.

"Not until you tell me what she said." Again, I couldn't believe my own stupidity. The first time anyone had asked me to dance and I was making the conditions.

"Come and dance and I'll tell you," he said.

"Okay," I warned, "but I'm a lousy dancer. I'll step on your feet and you'll be embarrassed to be dancing with me. People will laugh."

"I don't care a hoot about the laughter of people," he said, "and, honey, you shouldn't either."

He held out his arms and we started to dance. He looked down at me with those blue eyes.

"She said you were a pain in the ass, but the smartest girl in her bunk house," he told me.

That was too much to bear. I had almost become accustomed to meanness, but hearing something nice broke down all my defenses. I dashed outside so that nobody would see me crying. He followed.

"It must be pretty bad," he said gently.

"Please don't be nice to me, I'll just keep on crying."

Tears sloshed down my face and dripped onto the borrowed sweater. They had warned me about the mascara running, so I pulled a grubby Kleenex out of my pocket and wiped away the tears and half of the make-up.

He held out his arms. "Let's dance out here."

Maybe sarcasm would help me stop crying. "What is this?" I said, "be kind to fat girls night?"

"Honey," he smiled, "it's be kind to southern boys night."

I smiled. "I'll bet everyone is nice to you all the time."

"You'd lose the bet," he answered.

I liked his accent, the lazy, soft quality of his voice. Maybe this was the way Thomas Jefferson spoke. And he had good manners. I think this was the first time I had ever met anyone with good manners. Long afterward I read that good manners were making the other person feel comfortable.

"I'm sorry, but I don't know your name," I told him.

"Blaine," he said. "Blaine French. And your name is Katie Connor. Betsy told me."

"It was originally O'Connor," I said.

He threw back his head and laughed.

"Why is that funny?"

"It's your odd compulsion to be honest. I find that refreshing. What kind of girl are you? No coyness, no manipulations?"

"I don't know what you mean," I said.

"No, you probably don't. Let's just say there's a difference between you and that counselor of yours."

"Don't you like her?" I asked.

"I used to, but Betsy isn't very kind. One might call Betsy an experience."

How wonderful to have someone see things the way I did, to find an ally. Just knowing one person who understood that Betsy wasn't kind helped me to feel better. A lot of the summer's pain started to fade away.

"Where are you from," I asked him.

"New Hope, Georgia, the most boring little town in the entire United States."

"Watertown, Massachusetts is boring too," I said.

"But at least it's not dry."

"No," I agreed, "we get plenty of snow and rain."

He laughed again, gloriously, loudly. I had never seen anyone laugh that way before. In fact, as I watched him I realized that nobody in my family, except my grandmother and I, laughed at all. My mother glowered, my father tiptoed, Phillip studied and Maggie contently hummed along. My mother was always telling me "empty barrels make the most noise," when I dared to laugh out loud at home.

Blaine put his arms around me, ready to dance again. I shivered. Never before had anyone held me quite this way, in gentle friendliness. My usual embarrassment left me. If I stepped on his toes he didn't notice, and his light chatter covered any awkward gaps in the conversation.

"This is a waltz, honey," he said. "Don't pull away. That's right. Relax. Just kind of drift in my arms."

It was like when I learned to ride a two-wheeled bicycle. For a long time it seemed impossible and then, suddenly, I could do it, and I wondered why it seemed so hard in the first place.

I'm dancing, I thought. I'm dancing and having the best time of my life.

"Hold your head up," he said. "Why do you always look at your toes?"

It was impossible not to tell him the truth. "I'm ashamed of not being pretty."

He stopped dancing, put his hand under my chin, and studied my face seriously.

"I think you are pretty. It's a different kind of prettiness, but I like it."

"I don't usually look even this nice," I said. "Usually I look awful. This is the first time I've ever worn make-up, and these aren't my clothes. I had to borrow them because I don't have nice ones of my own."

"If that isn't just like me," he said. "I'm always misplacing things and having to borrow. I'm the absolute despair of my father. Even military school couldn't change me. And don't you worry none about adding that little bit of make-up. I become absolutely ugly by simply needing to shave."

"You couldn't look ugly," I said.

"Just watch." He screwed up his face and started to prance around like the phantom of the opera. I burst into laughter and enjoyed myself. I really did have a nice laugh, and I wasn't just being an "empty barrel."

"Just what is going on out there?" Betsy's cold voice splintered my laughter.

He limped over to her with his imitation hunchback walk, peered up at her, and said, "Haven't we met somewhere before?"

"Just how much have you had to drink tonight?" she snarled.

"Not as much as I would like to have, not as much as I want to have, not as much as I intend to have. Betsy, you're looking mighty lovely."

"I have been waiting inside for you," she said.

"I clean forgot," he said. "I guess there are some people who are just easy to forget."

Betsy gasped and for an instant I almost felt sorry for her. I guess his good manners were not always good. But I was too smart to take comfort from her humiliation. I knew I'd pay for witnessing it. She struggled to regain some kind of advantage.

"Am I to conclude that you have taken a fancy to children?"

"I don't notice any children here," he said. "I am just interacting with the pure of heart."

"Just see that you respect that purity," she said. "She's desperate for attention."

His voice mocked her. "Katie, honey, are you desperate for attention?"

"I don't get much," I said.

"Isn't that a coincidence. I'm starved for affection, too. Now, Betsy here is not starved for affection, because she never heard of it."

"I don't want to see you until you've sobered up," Betsy said. She turned and stalked angrily back into the hall.

"She'll get even with me for this," I said.

"If she does anything at all to make you unhappy, this is what you say, Katie. You ask, 'Is what Blaine told me about your first date true, Betsy?' I guarantee she'll deflate instantly."

"Why are you being so nice to me?" I asked.

"Because niceness is not wasted on you," he said.

Again, I wanted to cry. I was worried too. I kept glancing at the door to see if Betsy was watching us.

"I don't feel like dancing anymore," I said.

"My thoughts exactly. We'll go down to the lake and look at the moon. I assume you are a moon watcher. You wait right here while I get us some refreshments."

"But if you're in charge of the dance, don't you have to be there?" I asked.

"I try not to have to be anywhere. Now don't you go running off with anybody else. Promise?"

He darted off, quicksilver, Hermes, Mercury, a fleet-footed god.

I waited. What if he were making a fool of me. What if he didn't come back? Then I felt his hand on my shoulder, feeling warm right through the borrowed sweater.

"Had to sneak past old Betsy," he said. "I was honestly afraid she's cast an evil spell over us. I'm afraid of bad magic."

Bad magic? It couldn't compare with his good magic. He slowly walked ahead of me toward the waterfront.

The bright moon shone for us. Could this be the same lake I saw from the other side? All these weeks I'd been too depressed to contemplate its beauty.

We walked to the end of the wooden deck, and he put down a blanket he had been carrying. He reached into the water and pulled up a mesh sack with a bottle of beer inside it. He handed me the Coke he'd brought from the hall.

"We counselors are supposed to set a good example," he grimaced. "No beer, no liquor, no cigarettes."

"I don't like the smell of beer," I told him.

"Then what do you drink," he asked, "gin?"

I had no answer for that. My parents drank all the time at home. It always made me sad and angry to see them drink too much and then shout and yell at one another and me and to finally fall into an uneasy sleep.

Sitting there, with Blaine drinking beer and me sipping Coke, we were companionable and pleasant.

"How old are you?" he asked.

"Sixteen," I lied. "How old are you?"

"Eighteen."

Eighteen—that surprised me. He was younger than Betsy. It was unusual for girls to go out with boys who were younger than they were. But I suppose it was different at camp.

"Are you comfortable?" he asked.

Imagine someone caring enough about my comfort! I nodded, too touched to talk.

He lit a cigarette and leaned back on one elbow.

"Tell me about you," he said.

"What do you want me to tell you?" I asked.

"Everything. About your home, your parents, your life in Watertown." Even Watertown sounded beautiful when he said it.

"There's nothing to tell," I said. "Everything about my life is boring."

He grinned. I kept wondering why a I amused him so much, but I just accepted it for the moment. He made me feel very witty every time I said anything.

"There must be more to your life than that," he said. "I tell you what. You tell me about your life, and if you tell me enough, I'll tell you a little about mine."

"My life is absolutely awful," I began, noting again that he seemed to be amused. "I live in Watertown, in a terrible place quite close to the center of town, where there is nothing to do except listen to all the traffic from the square and go to school and church. My family lives on the first floor of a two story house, and it's always noisy. We can hear the people upstairs and the people next door—and the landlord is terrible. He and my parents don't talk to each other. He wants to get us out so that his relatives can move in. All winter long we freeze and in the summer it's so hot that we can't sleep. My mother wants to move some place where she can have her own house and garden. She likes to grow things. But it will never happen because we don't have any money.

"My father is a kind of accountant for a firm in Boston. He takes the bus every morning and again at night. Because he always rides at rush hour, he has to stand both ways, and he's exhausted when he gets home. He and my mother never kiss each other when he comes home or anytime. My mother is cracked on the subject of germs, and as soon as my father comes in at night, she makes him shower and change his clothes. She's afraid he'll bring home the plague or something."

"My brother is five years older that I am. I don't see him much, and when I do we don't have anything to say to each other. It's funny, but I have more to say to you. He goes to Dartmouth on a partial scholarship, but it's still a big expense for my folks. They're very proud of him. Do you really want to hear more?"

He nodded. He was gradually finishing the quart of beer. I wondered how anybody, outside of my parents could drink so much of that stuff.

"Then there's my little sister. She's five years younger than I am, so I can't really talk to her either. Besides, I don't like to talk to her because I am jealous of her. Everyone's always saying how adorable she is, how petite, how cute, how smart.

"My grandmother lives with us too. And there's only one bathroom. My mother has to schedule people like a traffic cop in the morning."

I stopped, suddenly embarrassed at having told him about the bathroom. Casually, he reached up and pulled me down beside him on the blanket, and put his arm under me.

"That's better," he said. "Now continue."

I could hardly talk. I was afraid my weight would break his arm. But it was wonderful being so close to another human being. I really didn't want to talk.

"I'm waiting," he said. His words sounded slurred.

"Well, my grandfather is dead and that's why my grandmother lives with us. She's my father's mother. She came from Prince Edward Island, Canada, and was a champion pig caller and butter churner when she was a girl living on her father's farm. She spent most of her savings to buy me a piano, because she thinks I have musical talent. She dusts the piano a lot, but I've never heard her play it. She says the piano is too good for her. But she loves music. I love her and she loves me, best of all. She does a lot of work for my mother, but my mother always makes her feel unwelcome. Whenever my mother is angry at my father, she scolds Gram. I'm sorry Gram doesn't have a place of her own."

"My grandmother sold all her furniture when she came to live with us, all except her bed and an old wooden rocker. She rocked me in it when I was little. Then, one day, my mother sold it. She said it was an eyesore. There was nothing Gram could do. She can't stand to think about that rocking chair."

"Now Gram has to perch on the edge of her bed in that cold room. She never complains, but I know she's lonely. We're a family of lonely people. My mother has made it that way. She has a way of making people lonely.

"Let's see . . . what else? I go to a Catholic school, get good grades, and I play the piano. I like to read. I have no friends. I never have any spending money, but I'll try to get a job when I get home. My goals are to have one close girlfriend, maybe someday a boyfriend, and to have a stereo and lots of classical records and lots of money for books."

He was silent. I looked at him and saw that he was asleep. I had done it again. Bored someone so much that all he could was fall asleep. I was feeling stiff and uncomfortable. I tried to move away, but he tightened his arms around me, pulled me to him and kissed me gently on the lips. My first kiss. Then he opened his eyes and smiled at me.

"You fell asleep," I said accusingly.

"Heard every word, honey," he said.

He sat up and lightly touched my hair.

"Now it's my turn," he said. "I turned eighteen just before the summer, and in September I'm going to enter college—William and Mary. I lived in New Hope, Georgia, where my father's family has lived for generations. And let me tell you, Watertown couldn't be as boring. In New Hope there's one hotel, one main street, a few stores, and then, nothing."

"My mother came from Savannah, and she never did adjust to New Hope. She died when I was twelve. She was what one might call a sporadic mother. No, that's not quite right. Indifferent isn't right either. I mean, when she was interested in me, which wasn't always, she gave me her full attention. With all the reading you've done, Katie, you can supply the right word."

I shook my head. But it seemed to me that a sporadic mother would be a great improvement over a mother like mine, who would never let you alone.

"My father is a lawyer, and his father and grandfather were lawyers also. Soon after my mother's death, I was sent to military school, and my father married his secretary. She is much younger than he is, and she didn't like his way of life, so she recently departed for parts unknown."

"Did you want to go to military school?" I asked.

"I'm afraid I had little choice in the matter. My father sent me away because my stepmother did not care for children."

"I think that's terrible," I said indignantly. "Even though my mother seems to hate us sometimes, she still seems to want us around."

He laughed, and I suddenly felt guilty.

"Listen," I said. "You aren't going to tell anyone any of the things I told you today about my family, are you? I mean, I wouldn't want Betsy and the other girls to know how terrible my life is."

"You have to trust some people, Katie," he said. "You have to be able to take some risks without caring what other people think. But if it will reassure you, I'll tell you some of my own deep, dark secrets."

I waited curiously. At that moment, I found it difficult to believe that beautiful people had problems.

"When I arrived at military school I was completely lost. The strangeness of the place and my own loneliness caused what they called a nervous breakdown. The school authorities sent for my father and my mother to take me home. Do you know what happened then?"

I shook my head.

"They refused to come. My father said that he had paid the year's tuition and that my mental and physical health were the school's responsibility."

"I can't believe that," I said indignantly, yet believing it. "So what happened?"

"I recovered. Isn't that obvious? I recovered and I grew up and here I am today."

"That's a terrible story," I said.

"I knew you'd feel that," he said. "As soon at Betsy pointed you out to me, I recognized in you a fellow sufferer."

"Well, I am a fellow sufferer, that's true. But it's only part of it. You, at least, are good looking and popular. You have your own crowd. I have to be miserable all alone."

"I'm all alone, too," he said. He wasn't smiling now.

"What happened next?" I asked.

"I went through school. My father's marriage ended, but it didn't interfere too much with his way of life. He drinks. He plays golf. He gets through time. He believes he is setting me a fine example."

"Even though my parents sometime drink a lot, I know drinking isn't a good example," I said.

"True, but drinking in New Hope is the town's major source of entertainment. Without liquor, no one could endure New Hope. My father schedules his life around the bottle. He rises and has a drink with his breakfast. He arrives at his office, shaved, well dressed, the very model of a Southern gentleman. During the day he has some more drinks. At dusk, he returns home to drink, and after dinner he cradles his bottle until he gropes his way to bed."

"Of course he is not exactly the best company. Feeling an overwhelming need to escape for a summer, I read the camp couselor positions in the *New York Times*, and here I am."

He got up and walked over to the waterfront bathroom. When he came back, he leaned over the dock and pulled up another bag with a bottle.

"I'm cagey," he said. "If they find one bottle, they won't think to look for a second one."

I nodded as if I understood. "Maybe we'd better go," I said.

He looked at his watch. "Plenty of time. It's only nine-thirty. I won't let you miss your bus."

His speech was more than a little slurred. Was he getting drunk? Could you get drunk from beer? I didn't know. Perhaps he was just tired.

"My mother was a pretty woman," he continued, "as I remember her." He sounded sad now. "Pretty, fragile, slim, gentle."

What marvelous words! I'd die happy if anyone described me that way.

"I told you how she didn't like New Hope. By the time I was ten, she was drinking heavily. And she wasn't strong. Just getting dressed for the evening, fixing her hair, deciding what dress to wear—every moment seemed to tire her. Her hands would flutter up to her hair, then down again. Even breathing seemed to be an effort."

"What did she die of," I asked.

"Cancer. I guess she was sick with it for a long time. Maybe that was why she drank. It must be very difficult to be hopelessly sick. I guess if I were to describe my mother in one word it would be 'tired.' "

I thought for a moment about my mother, I guess the one word I would use to describe her would be angry."

"Because I didn't know how sick she was," he went on, "sometimes I would be very angry with her for drinking. She drank vast quantities of sherry. She always had a glass of sherry beside her, even in the morning."

"Didn't that interfere with her housework?" I asked.

"No, we had a housekeeper. We have had the same housekeeper for thirty years."

I was really impressed. Nobody I knew had a housekeeper. Before my brother graduated from high school, my mother got a cleaning woman to come in and help her, but otherwise she and Gram did all the housework. In fact, my mother was the kind of person who would make a point of doing housework even when she was sick, to make us feel guilty.

"Didn't your father know how sick she was?" I asked.

"I don't think he knew. But he wasn't angry with her for drinking. They seemed to love each other a great deal. He delighted in her. She was at one time a great beauty."

He was quiet, his arms around his knees, his eyes looking out at the moon on the lake. He gave a little sigh. Was he crying? Impossible. I had never seen a man cry, not anywhere except in the movies. Timidly, I touched his face. He was crying! Awkwardly I patted his back and offered him my grubby Kleenex. I guess he was a little drunk. Would I cry over the death of my mother? I hoped God wouldn't punish me if I secretly thought I'd feel liberated. No, that's not true. I didn't want my mother to die. I just wanted her to evaporate, to go someplace else.

"We'd better go back," he said. "I don't want you to get in trouble."

"That's okay," I assured him. "Everybody hates me anyway."

"Oh, Katie." He was laughing again. "Nobody hates you."

He put his arms around me and gave me a brotherly hug. We stood there, comforting each other for a few minutes, then we started back.

He held my hand as we walked. We were friends. We stood at the door of the bus and beamed at each other. I was glad we weren't late. People were streaming out of the hall and onto the bus, so we had to talk fast.

"I'm off a week from Saturday night," he said. "I'll borrow a car and pick you up outside your camps' sign. You know the archway with the big "Camp Mickmack" on it. I'll have to wait until lights out—say about ten twenty. You'll be able to walk to the road, won't you? It shouldn't take you more than fifteen or twenty minutes, but take a flashlight. If there's a no moon, you won't be able to see."

"Oh, god," I said. "I can't do that. I'd get in trouble. I'd be afraid. They'd kick me out of camp. They'd call my mother or something. I just don't think I could do it."

"Katie, honey," he said wearily, "if you won't do a thing to help yourself, don't complain about how terrible things are for you. I thought you'd want to see me again."

"Of course, I do," I said. "This has been the best night of my life. Don't you know that?"

"Then meet me," he said.

Betsy was coming. I didn't want her to see me standing there talking to him.

"Okay, okay. I'll be there." I got into the bus.

My cabinmates piled into the bus and rushed to surround me.

"What's he like?" Andy asked. "Where'd he go?"

"Boy, was Betsy mad," Pat whispered. "She was twitching all over the place looking for you. Uh-oh, here she comes."

Betsy sat down in front of me as the bus started off. "And where, may I ask, were you all evening?" She began.

"You may not ask," I said. I think I was as shocked as she was by my answer.

"If Mrs. Donahue knew, you would not be permitted to go to future dances," Betsy said. "It's strictly against the rules to leave the hall."

"I didn't know that," I said. "But you didn't have to worry, Betsy. I was with a friend of yours."

An angry exhalation of breath, a sudden wilting and she sank back into her seat. Pat squeezed my hand. Things were looking up.

Sara Hunter

A LESSON IN FACING

The dog barked once,
we felt a lurch against the house,
and the first great bird
came dragging along the grass,
feathers like banana leaves, claws like dragons.

The seed-bell went in one quick peck.
The dog snapped next in the long, purple beak.
Cracking the window, but too big to squeeze through,
his head halved the living room, almost taking you.

The next bird shuddered down on the roof,
the third one tapped out the kitchen glass,
the fourth closed the way to the west,
the fifth blocked the eastern porch.

That was the coming of the first great birds.
We lived entrapped for more than a week.
Then we learned the trick of the sacrifice:
We offered them our babies, one by one.

Daniel went, and then Delilah.
Christopher cried, and we held him back.
On the tenth day, the birds departed,
leaving the stink of our cowardice.

At the next coming, we walked out to meet them,
Christopher riding on your back.
The great bird bowed, they do not devour
what comes forward, even in fear.

SPIDER CONTRACT

O spider, you may live with me,
but not in my bed.
Jump off! Go to a corner!
I will host you all winter
if you are circumspect.
I will ladder you up with a towel
if you fall in the tub.
But do not crawl over me,
stay off my pillow.
Ten legs
are too many
in one bed.

THE ANT-SLAYER

Talking with someone I thought I would like,
a man praised by my friends,
he asked what I called them,
the large, soldier ants,
said, "How I hate them, the nasty things!"
crushing one with a self-approved grin
as if he had slain a dragon.

I, who break crusts
into ant-hole-sized millicrumbs,
I, who sidestep their small, earnest crawlings,
I, with my secretly segmented nature,
scurried my six-legged soul into hiding!

THE GOOD FAIRIES GIVE GIFTS
AT THE BIRTH OF FUTURE PHYSICIAN (MALE)

We wish for this child
one migraine, one labor,
one hemorrhagic period,
one stroke confusing his words,

one day of blindness,
one of deafness,
one paralysis,
one amputation,

one schizophrenic episode,
one day of psoriasis,
one loss of a child,
and one hospitalization—emergency,
and without insurance.

Then let him heal himself
and others.

AT AN INFANT'S WAKE

Uncrying, unkicking, unclenching,
unsucking, unhungry, unwarm,
    still soft
    still round
    still silk-skulled
                  still dead.
what power and grief
pervade this baby's head!

THE SENSITIVE ACCOUNTANT'S APPROACH

Let me kiss the eight interstices of your toes,
the six of your fingers
and the double webs of your thumbs.
Let me trace the six lines of your palms,
the two that encircle your throat,
and the clusters that bloom from your eyes,
clocking innumerable smiles.
Let my arms measure the curve of your ribs,
and my fingers caress all your vertebrae.
Let me bless doubly your breasts and your lips,
and quadruply, the four-lipped entrance.

UGLY DUCKLINGS AND FAKE SWANS

Ugly, bulky, no-neck, scowling kid,
hard to see swan in you, swan-soul,
no one did.
I saw the bully that my sister was
and thought no more about you, crossed you out.

But when they beat you, it was me you called
to witness and to get the doctor in,
trusting in my hidden duckliness,
I, long-necked, with power to protect
and power—somehow you guessed—to penetrate
what floated quietly within and deeply hid:
that white and graceful self, your slender soul.

DECIDING ON SPECIES

If the burden
is much bigger than my body,
I must be an ant.

But if I carry it alone,
I must be human.

If I leave the burden behind,
I must be an angel.

But if all burdens load me,
I am God.

OUTSIDE THE DANCE

for B.B.

I saw them standing outside the dance.
It was not with me they were going to dance.
My mother wouldn't let me dance.
I said, "But there's a boy!" She kept me in
to punish me for wanting boys, for wanting more
than mother had, and younger, too, I wanted it:
what boys and girls did, why they danced.

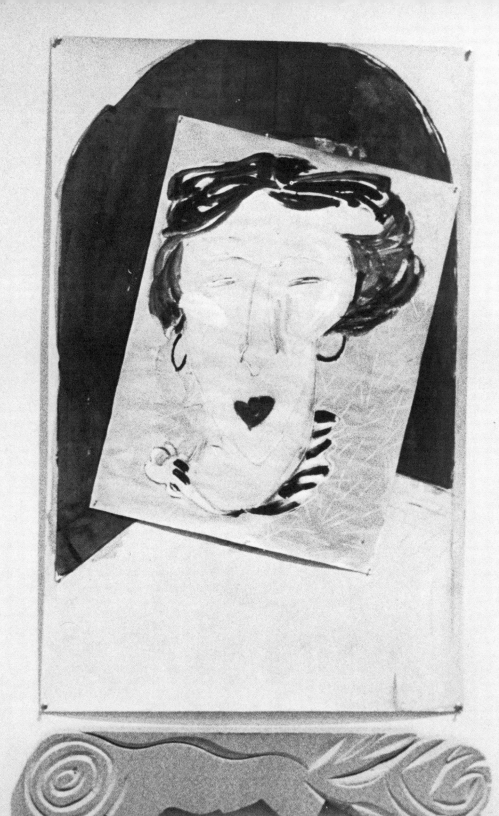

Constance Egemo

WAITING FOR THE MEN TO RETURN

Often on winter evenings during the war
mother would sit to one side of the hearth,
my sisters around her,
and, perched on the small mahogany rocker,
I would unpin her hair.
I would hold her long brown hair in my hands,
I would lift it and turn it under the brush,
inhaling its animal odor,
and I watched the firelight move down its length as I brushed.
Sparks leaped from her head into the darkness
and I felt the shock of that power she carried on her head,
an energy old as fire yet more hidden,
controlled by pins and ribbons,
held in all day to halo her head,
but loosened at night, falling into its own,
and breathing a foreign resonance into the room,
a deep antipathy against the background
of all that sweet genre music.

In the safe indoor world of home
we bathed away sweat, put on clean clothes,
ate in a mannerly way, smiled at each other,
pulled back our caramel braids, were polite to our elders,
but her fierce primitive hair, unpinned, gave us away.
In the firelight my sisters and I knew
that we were the same as our mother.
The men were off fighting a war
yet here by the hearth we harbored a secret power
that made us all witches at the roots of our hair,
for we bore in our bodies
the deep fragrant sources of womanhood.

And my mother would smile under the stroking brush.
She would reach up dreamily

to smooth back the hair at her temples
and tell us about her childhood.
"My mother's hair was black," she said,
"so long that when she let it down, she could sit on it.
On summer days I would brush it in our garden.
She was almost forty then, but her skin was white as milk.
When the young men of the village walked by,
they would stop and suck in their breaths."

ITEM/MINNEAPOLIS STAR AND TRIBUNE

they found another woman in
the river   no one
knows who she was   they can't be
sure how old   45 to 60 years
water changes things   age
changes things   she was five feet
six inches   weighed one hundred thirty
pounds and had brown hair   blue
eyes   she was wearing a gold
wedding band and a mother's ring with
a cluster of three
stones   anyone with information about
this woman   45 to 60 years
medium height   medium
weight   three children   who was
wearing green slacks   a red shirt and
a brown overcoat found on
the Cedar Avenue bridge please
contact the medical examiner's office
please contact   please
no one knows who she was

AS I WALKED OUT

As I walked out of the funeral home where my father lay,
I didn't pause in contemplation of death.
I didn't wonder whether the last sleep
falls on the mind as softly as all the others.
My eyes found nothing to hold them,
nothing in the dark splashes of juniper by the stairs,
nor in the gravel path through the courtyard,
nor in the gray stone bench, stolid under the leafless maple.

Then I saw that someone had taken the roof off the sky.
Where there had been stars and moon,
where clouds had drifted,
there was only a black corridor stretching endlessly out,
darker than any black I'd ever known,
a cruel, empty black, a vacuum like nightmare.

And suddenly, as I stood looking up,
I saw flashes of light from the branches of the maple tree,
thin, urgent fingers reaching upward with a low crackling.
The tree was on fire; I saw it flickering,
water-blue, sky-blue, yet blue burning.
As a tree burgeons with flowers in spring,
the maple blazed with spirit foliage,
pale leaves and blossoms uttering speech against the night.

I looked down at the ground.
A pulsing shell of light surrounded the juniper boughs
and the light whispered; I heard its voice.
The rocks also shone, the light not leaping from them
but glowing in blue embers.
And the bench gave off light;
I saw the stones like ingots shining and singing together,
and the energy ascended into the air,
into the black corridor overhead,
the limitless emptiness, the stark roofless sky.

LIKE A BIRD BUILDS ITS NEST

It's winter. I can't rest in this house.
I want to put things away.
I need to find order around me.
I feel like a cat swollen with young,
prowling to find a warm corner.
My grandmother always used to say
in the spring you clean for birth,
in the fall for death. It's winter
and yet I'm getting my house ready.

Something is coming that I can't name.
Its shadow looms in my sleep
and I lie restless, listening.
At night the chairs and tables stand
stiffly in place like sentinels waiting
and the upstairs timbers explode with cold.
In the spring, in the fall, I have always
straightened and readied my house
but this year something comes out of season.

Grandmother always said you clean
like a bird builds its nest,
because you can't help it,
and I know it's winter, the wrong season,
yet I can't keep calm, I must be ready,
I *will* have order in all my house.
Some advent is moving to flood
and I'm getting my house ready
but there is no wise woman now to tell me why.

MIDWESTERN TRUCK STOP
WITH FARMERS DRIVING BACK FROM TOWN

I love to sit in the smell of men
    come in from their trucks,
men who think with their bodies,
whose gestures are their perfect voice,
whose minds are not tied up with inner arguments,
who jump down from their trucks in the cold,
    steam rising from their bodies,
who swagger into cafés,
whose shoulders struggle against their seams,
whose voices are too large for small rooms,
whose fingers are criss-crossed with scars,
whose nails are broken by use,
who comb their hair in the morning
    and sometimes again at night,
who throw themselves into squealing chairs
    and huffle into their coffee,
who snort and slap their knees when they laugh,
who swipe at their mouths with their sleeves,
who rise from tables with exaggerated care
    and plow deeply back into their jackets,
who toss change carelessly onto tables,
who makes jokes as they pay their bills,
who are mightily amused by waitresses,
and who plunge back into parking lots,
    toothpicks dangling from their lips,
    their necks already craning toward home.

JOCASTA

patience my
ass   she said
her left hand swept
upward

we were on a
hillside drinking
bourbon and the white
dandelion heads exploded
under her
gesture

she was lying
in the grass   her gypsy
skirt rucked up
to her hips

he can't fuck   she
said and the clover
shook under her
sobs
I've been his mother
too long   she said

I'm going out and strangle
someone

THE SWIMMER

I wake suddenly,
knowing he's there.
My son stands near the door,
his knees flexed, his arms bent.

In my bedroom in moonlight
he floats in the substance
of his dream.

Now he listens with his forehead
as he used to before he was born.
Now he remembers when his only speech
was a soft dance under my belly.

In his sleep he has come
searching for me
to witness the secret world he explores,
and I dare not help him
nor bring him back.

Now, slowly, he reaches up
and questions the air with a gesture.
His hand moves toward something
only he can see.

His fingers open
and remain outspread,
as though he petitions some gift
from darkness.

Now he stares at his hand in awe,
silent, motionless in the still night,
and he takes in his breath
deeply, deeply.

In the moonlight his body,
unfinished as eggwhite,
becomes opaque, straightens,
changes as I watch.

In his chest,
the long dream of the world
opens.

And my son,
smiling with dream knowledge
turns away from me and walks
into another room.

HEARTLAND

My son who hunts
is haunted.
This year his father
taught him to shoot wild geese.
They fly back in dreams,
crying out to him in human voices,
dying again and again
on the bedroom floor.

Sue Ann Martinson

JUNCTURE

one small daffodil emerges
moon yellow
framed by a pale stucco house

surrounded by still frozen
ground and snow flecked
with earth and soot

no one ever said it would
come to this
turn

in the world's holocaust of ideas
this reign of intellectual terror
thrust with malice everywhere
only nature brings solace

weeds have no conscience, but are
life, real and sprawling
nor do stars
they move predictably, abstract,
glittering, toward no destination

of star, of weed
of a single moon-yellow daffodil
that sing with no sound we can hear

UPPER HENNEPIN AVENUE

the rooms above Mousey's Bar
a sunny fall afternoon

she leans out the window
her body thrust forward
and spits
onto the sidewalk

she settles back in her blue nightgown
that matches her pale skin
caught between the window frame
and a white sheet curtain

I want to be a photographer
a painter, anyone who can
capture her face
skewed at once in pain and sadness
she is not young, she is not old
she carries her years like
extreme unction

her lips are all angles, out of
proportion, like a cubist painting
her hair brown, soft, looks like
she just washed and curled it
but it has no fire, like her
face, her body, passive
disappointed, resigned

I want to rush to her and say
No, you don't have to stay here.
It's not even where the
classy hookers hang out

I am trapped in the bus
as it moves past the brick
and movie marquees of Hennepin Avenue

she'd probably say
"Who the hell are you?"

MOON

of stone   water   fire   blood
you make children grow inside women
plants come to life
earth sister, earth mother
yellow-gold cosmic egg, seed of the world
Queen of the Bright Night and Darkness
guide to the lost traveller
pathway to visions, sleep, and death
spirit of the underworld, ruler of madness
home of the dead awaiting rebirth
home of souls unborn
Queen of Dreams
You rise from death to fire

INTERLUDE

on the edge
between darkness and light

my life, like tatting
looped and looped again
interlocking threads
the heart fiber

I do not believe in the pot of gold
at the end of the rainbow
I do believe in rainbows
rain-glass prisms that hold the light

I go where I wish, when I wish
create patterns, small steps:

> Someone once told me that knowledge is like climbing a moun-
> tain—we follow a path, footsteps carved by those who have
> gone before. And I thought, can I make my own small steps?
> Leave my imprint? So Emily Dickinson carved her own
> delicate steps, Madame Curie, Georgia O'Keefe.

It has not always been this easy,
nor will be again,
to see my life so clearly:

My wealth is in the rain stepping lightly over the grass
in those whose hearts I share, in the fall of light
the sun weaving its rays through an afternoon,
laughter falling through a roomful of strangers,
a gathering of friends

like tatting thread, I loop and loop again
make patterns of air for light to shine through
rainbows of lace, the heart fiber

ALLEGRO RISOLUTO

signs on the wind
imprint of crows' feet
the shadows of the days are longer

I do not recognize myself in the mirror
the small eyes, severe face

I am almost forty
yesterday I was twenty
the years have etched themselves on a pane of glass
translucent, I look as through a mirror:
I am young and slim, angry and sad

always, I have turned to the wind
sought the grass the sky the water
these have been my resting places
alone, I have sought the solace of wind and rain
I do not fear the lightning

in my dreams I catch falling stars
I hold the moon in my palm
my heart has not changed
I learn to wear my new body with grace

Marcia Jagodzinske

SEEDS

Out in the community gardens
my husband and I
push dirt
and dream of self-sufficient
basement shelves
crammed with shiny
lidded jars.

We plot our rows
carefully.
We companion plant,
we mulch,
we use wood ash,
we water.

Friday nights
used to be for dancing
and eating
tender seafood
dipped in butter.
Now we watch slides
on the iris
and hope to win
a door prize.
Maybe some seeds
or even a garden hose.

We have become our parents
and our grandparents.
It is hard to say
anymore
whether we are young
or much too old.

AFTER THE WEDDING

My mother phones
to see how I am.

She doesn't want
to know
the dishrag stories
conjured in
incantations
over a steaming
wedding cake.

Doesn't want to know
things don't change.
That her granddaughters
will grow up
with tattooed bodies.
Second class
citizens.

Doesn't want to know
women still die
in childbirth
and the world
celebrates
a male birth.

Doesn't want
to be told
we are both
property
of our spouses.

Doesn't like to see
that death
can be less painful
for women
than living.

I tell her
I'm fine.

THE MARRIAGE

He touches
the deep spaces
between my shoulders
and moves
where there is no light.

It is a relationship
bound by silver
and relatives
on each side
of the family.

I ask him to buy milk.
He brings home dreams
on raffle tickets.

He buys a Christmas wreath
for a worthy cause
and forgets to pick up eggs.

I am hungry with him.
I am bones and flesh
without.

THE ELECTRICIAN

To him
there is no place
so safe
as a maze of wires
turning things off
keeping things on.
He carries batteries
in his pockets
and flosses his teeth
with stripped wire.

At night
his wife turns him on
and he dances for her
like a twinkle light
propped upon
a Christmas tree.

THE HOOKER

She lays down
in narrow spaces
and offers up her legs
to men
with cold belt buckles
and food
between their teeth.

She lets them think
she likes them.

In her mind
she castrates them
and they walk away
imaginary cripples.

She feeds their sperm
to stray dogs
with long tongues
and watches
immortality die.

Donna Nitz Muller

COMMON GROUND

Knee deep in the dry, scratchy grass, Carla tugged with her toes until she had a spot of bare, black earth large enough for her whole foot to burrow into the coolness.

The heat was heavy on her eyelids. The taste of dust clung to her mouth and nose. When she pivoted on her buried foot the cool dirt stuck between her toes. With her eyes she followed the thin pencil mark of earth and sky which encircled all she knew.

A sweet calmness existed out here, a mile ride from the house and many miles from any other place. There was no worry about saying the wrong thing or trying to talk at all. The endless space on all sides of everything could not be held accountable for the blankness in Carla's mind every time she was spoken to directly.

At fourteen she blamed herself. Deep sobs would push out from her stomach and end, silenced, in her throat. Carla believed herself mysteriously disfigured. Something hidden from her own eyes, but obvious to everyone around her.

Once when Carla was a sophomore her father drove her the six miles into town. He left her off at the gym for a dance featuring a band from Sioux Fall. The excitement in the air penetrated her skin, pumping energy through her veins.

She watched her father make a u-turn on the street and start for home. She was to stay overnight with a friend. It was arranged. Clapping her hands and turning with a light bounce, Carla ran for the door and the sound of bursting from inside.

The girls moved around in pastel colored, box-pleated skirts and matching sweaters which gave their hips a nice fullness and their breasts a soft presence. The boys stood in clusters like planets held together by an invisible force.

Carla stood by the door looking for her friend. She wasn't a close friend, but her mother had made a call to the girl's mother. It was fine for Carla to come home with her friend. After several minutes Carla moved to wait on the bleachers. She watched as the boys began to shake loose from their groups and pull sparkling bits of color out of a colored cloud.

No one approached her. She saw no one she dared join with some silly joke and shake of flipped-up hair. Never had the prairie been this lonely, this void of company.

Carla began to feel that scratchy burn behind her eyes, so she walked slowly with her head high and stomach in, to the entry for a drink. A young man from her bus stood with his friends by the fountain. Carla decided she was not thirsty, but the young man moved aside with a great show of courtesy as though she were a movie star. Carla's cheeks burned. She understood the laughter in his eyes. She knew they could see her disfigurement.

She walked home. In the cool darkness she followed the creek bed. It was October, the water had not yet frozen into solid ripples. Compared to the music which swelled her veins, the water cooled her, calmed her shaking hands.

Her own skirt was made from a wool material of expensive quality ordered special by a fabric center in Sioux Falls. The fit was perfect with the pleats swaying from her round hips. Her mother could sew with a professional talent. This skill was lost on Carla. Anything lovely was a waste on her. Carla knew this. The knowledge forced from her throat gulping sobs which would have broken anyone's heart if they had heard. No one heard. Her comfort was in the moon-lit sky and grassland space. People here did not plow the prairie.

Nothing much was said when Carla entered the house. She was fed some bacon and eggs. Her father kissed the top of her head. That was all. She noticed through the following weeks that her mother did not call the mother of her friend or go to her house for club, nor did Carla ask to go out.

Carla graduated from a private girl's college in Yankton. The graduation exercises were brief because of the heat. It was early May, 1969 and even on the peaceful, green slopes of the campus grounds a tension could be felt running as an invisible current. The tension moved through Carla because it moved through everyone. A nameless restlessness which was counted on as a part of college life in that year.

After lunch with her parents, Carla shut her suitcase on the blank, white stare of her diploma. She put the suitcase and her guitar into the back seat of the new Ford Mustang her parents gave her as a gift. She hugged each of them and told them not to worry. She had to find herself. Her father shook his head, and her mother assured her that they trusted her. They would not worry.

Carla guided her car across the bridge into Nebraska. The landscape sloped and rose like a pleasant, slow-motion roller coaster. Carla rolled down her window to allow the wind to blow her hair fiercely back from her high cheekbones. The miles moved past her, around her as though she were a force slicing through any resistance.

Sitting on the sidewalk of the truck stop outside Norfolk was a young man. He rested against a green duffle bag and looked anemic. Carla saw him and pulled to stop at the curb. She tightened her grip on the wheel and sternly reminded herself that from this moment on she was a new person. She would not be afraid because she would not let anything really matter.

She sat beside him, matching his slouch, elbows on her knees, "Do you need a ride?" He nodded. Carla, staring at his short hair, continued, "I have a car, but I don't have money. If you can buy the gas, I'll drive anywhere." Without looking at her, the man answered, "Sioux Falls." Carla shrugged. She had just left the state behind, but that didn't matter either. "Okay," she told him.

The young man sat with his knees against the dash and his head back, resting against the seat. His head turned toward the window, so Carla could not tell if he slept or studied the new deep shades of green. They moved north on highway 81 along a stretch of road where passing was impossible. She slowed from seventy-five to forty and rested her elbow along the window ledge.

They slowed down because of the green army truck with tarps flapping in the wind. The young man straightened, "A load of ammo, I bet, in that deuce and a half." Carla jumped at the unexpected sound. He had a low, rich voice like a performer on stage. "What?" she answered, her own voice scratchy. "It's a two ton truck carrying ammunition," he told her with some interest in his eyes. "Ick," her mouth a disapproving line.

"I've been there. Just left Saigon day before yesterday. We were hassled at the airport and snuck through entry like criminals. If you have a problem with that, I'll get out right here," he did not raise his voice. The anger made it a near whisper and turned his dark eyes almost black.

Where had the antagonism come from? She looked at her lap as though she might possibly be able to see the source somewhere in her stomach. "I'm sorry," Carla mumbled though she wasn't sure what she had done or if she should be sorry.

"What are you sorry about?" he questioned with a touch of wonder lacing the angriness of his tone.

"I am allowed to be sorry for you and for them and for us if I want to," Carla answered, feeling a little ruffled herself. It came as a shock to meet a soldier. She had held her sign demanding peace and love until everyone else went to the tavern for a beer. She still wore her slim, gold POW bracelet. In her spot under the bottom floor stairs she had prayed from an end to the war. For days after seeing photographs taken in Viet Nam she had not been able to eat. With every bite she saw those emaciated bodies and ghost-like eyes.

He made her feel alienated, lost as though she were not capable of touching him. "I was left in the hallway once by a blind date. He took one look at me and walked out. I didn't mind not going out as much as the desk clerk looking at me with that pathetic sympathy," she said it. The words could not be retrieved, drawn back inside. She saw surprise in his eyes. Her hands felt cold and her face burned.

"I was the only one to walk out from a fire fight after Charlie hit us on a hill we took three times." His voice was soft now. He didn't say it to see sympathy on her cheeks. He said it because it was there, behind his eyes.

The picture he drew with his words and his hands moving from his knees to his face silenced them both. It filled the small car and put such a weight on Carla's heart that her stomach lurched. She bit back any show of sympathy, forcing her features to be clear, expressionless. It had been the worst to look out from her shame and see those sorry faces.

"It is alright to suffer." Carla's voice was calm. She had already spoken too much, exposed herself and her secret to this stranger. Nothing more was to be lost by saying what occurred to her. "I mean there is nothing wrong with feeling pain inside. The hard part is to make it all right. To feel that it is worth something."

She stopped, shutting her lips tight against her teeth. Vince studied her profile for several minutes. He nodded and turned back to the window.

Carla's second trip over the bridge was made after dark. The bridge was bright from rows of lights so that it appeared to anticipate a crowd, but it was only the truck and her own car using all that light.

"Would you like a beer?" he asked her. Her heart pounded. It couldn't be helped. She felt the thumps within her chest and at the base of her throat. "With me?" her voice squeaky and sounding in her ears as though it belonged to someone else. Again he studied her with the expression of a man who had forgotten that people play games with each other. "You are different. I will give you credit for being different," he answered with the barest smudge of a smile at the corners of his mouth. Carla saw the approval of her in his look. She smiled.

Vince guided her by her elbow to a back booth in the tavern. Even before they reached the high-backed, plastic seats Carla felt anxious. The college boys wore their hair so long it easily parted at their shoulders. She had never really noticed this before, but now she turned nervous eyes to the bare suggestion of black hair on Vince's head. She wished she had driven to the uptown bar.

It was too late. As Vince slid in the booth across from her, Carla felt a quiet around them. She was afraid to look. Instead she raised her eyes to Vince's face. His expression was calm. No trace of impending disaster was noticeable in his eyes. She watched his chin tighten and felt her own hands turn into hard fists on her lap.

Charles Waxton, a quarterback from Yankton College, pulled up a chair as though greeting an old friend. Yankton possessed the unique distinction of having two colleges. Carla's alma mater stood in direct opposition to Yankton College in all things except general rebellion. As Charles sat down there was a slow rise of shadows around them.

She saw Vince inhale through his nose and exhale through an O shape of his mouth. Then he turned cold eyes toward Charles Waxton.

"So," Charles said through a big grin, "who have you killed lately?"

There wasn't the slightest change of expression on Vince's face. His mouth opened and the words dropped one by one from between his teeth, "I know who might be the next one."

Charles stood, tipping his chair over, and grabbed at Vince's green jacket. As Charles bent to pull Vince from his seat, Vince sent him to the floor with one chop of his hand.

Carla swallowed bitter tasting fluid which rose in her throat as she stared at the sprawled figure. He lay like a stupified drunk weakly flapping his hands.

"They taught you that?" she whispered to Vince.

"They had to or I would be dead," he answered her.

"My God," formed on her lips.

Carla looked up to see a ring of wide-eyed kids. The girls began to move back, and the boys were taking small, sliding steps toward them. At that moment Carla realized she possessed something which she would never have thought possible. Once she was beyond caring about being liked, she held a unique forcefulness. She was not afraid, so, she stood. Vince rose slowly to stand beside her. She took his arm, and the two of them began to walk from their booth.

It happened that as they took their first steps Carla caught the eye of a boy who had once stood through Medieval History rather than take the only empty seat. The seat was the one next to her. She saw his mouth as though it was the only thing visible in a black world. She saw it form the word, "bitch." Carla dropped her hand from Vince's arm as anger pulsed through her and forced tears.

She did not even take a breath. There was no thought, only a response of her body to that flowing, hot anger. Carla moved the four steps between them without knowing it. She saw the mouth with its full sneer and pulled back her elbow in order to cover that sneer with her soft fist. Her ears filled with an uproar. She felt the soft flesh of his lips over the hard teeth and pain shot to her shoulder.

The uproar grew stronger, hurting her ears like a pressure from within. It was only as she turned to find Vince that she saw various postures of open-mouthed laughter. Even Vince, his head slightly tilted toward one shoulder, was grinning at her. He held out a hand to her. She grabbed for it, and, reaching it, turned again to make sense from what she saw. Blood was dripping off the end of his chin like a baby who tried to drink milk from a glass.

Focusing around her, Carla understood at last. She had been funny. Her punch had caused all this laughter. She looked at Vince, directly into the deep brown of his eyes. He understood, and, placing her hand on his forearm under his own, led her from the tavern.

"He called me a bitch," she told him in tones of self-defense.

"I heard him," Vince answered.

"You mean he said it out loud?"

"Vince shook his head, "Of course he did, everyone heard him."

"I didn't hear him. I only saw his mouth."

When they reached the car, Carla gestured for him to drive. She stood in the cool air inhaling long breaths. Her whole body was shaking. She had never known such anger. It was, she decided, as they say, a boiling point, a blind rage. As it eased, the single rage of her life, a lightness took over her muscles. A weight was gone from her like walking on the moon.

Carla leaned on her elbow watching Vince sleep. His hair struggled to lay flat, but could only manage a slightly relaxed stand. Carla restrained herself from pulling his hair. Short hair was like a war cry. The short hairs against the throngs of long hairs screaming for justice without giving any. And she had to admit to being a long hair, a love-sick child. "But I didn't know," she mumbled, "I did not realize it was boys fighting that war. Poor scapegoat," and she bent to kiss his forehead.

He awoke. Instantly he grabbed behind his head, "Damn cong."

"No, it's me," fear in her voice.

"Oh, ya," he answered without apology. He was a mass of hardened scar tissue, rumpled and tough under her fingers. Carla would hate to be his enemy.

Vince loved her in an eruption of emotion. It amazed Carla, left her washed over with a tremendous compliment. "You know," he told her, "the funny thing about you is that you really are beautiful." Carla instinctively checked for laughter, for a secret joke. She found sincerity which touched her so deeply she closed her eyes to it.

"Wear your hair so that people can see your eyes. You have great eyes. They express your thoughts like green crystal balls." He laughed at her blush creeping up her neck and moving like fingers across her cheeks.

Without any demand in his fingers, he caressed her. "I noticed right away how straight you sit. Your shoulders hold up your great boobs." Carla could not bear to hear it. She turned away from him. He moved also. Nothing touched about them.

"You think you are so ugly so people think so too. But I'm telling you different. You are beautiful, and I've seen a lot of women." His words hovered in the hushed morning light. He lay on his back and directed his sentences to the pale green ceiling. Carla tried to swallow the sound of her crying. She couldn't.

For several minutes Vince stared at the ceiling while Carla fought to stop crying. She wondered why he didn't leave. Finally she asked him. "Because," he told her without movement except for his mouth, "I wish I could do that. Just lay in a motel room and cry. I wish I could."

Carla did not move either, "We are like *two lost privates* who become friends instead of shooting each other. We are like that." She turned to him and rested a cool, soft hand on his chest.

James Agnew

BURNING YOUR LETTER AT THE KITCHEN STOVE

I burn your letter
At the kitchen stove,
Starting with the corner.
The flames erase your signature
Cauterizing even the word "love."

Stretching up, the fire
Finds substance in my fingers.
It consumes my hand,
My wrist, my arm, my shoulder.
My body burns in the kitchen,
Still holding the empty phone
And this burning promise of a letter.

The fire spreads across the telephone wires
Destroying every house in this exchange.
Flames form pillars and whirlwinds,
Igniting everything in their dance.

The city burns, except, of course,
Your building. Apartment 38 stands
Untouched, with a forceful solemnity,
In the middle of endless constructions of flame.

Within, icy and safe from all this
You carefully compose your next letter.

SUMMER

The curve of summer
Cool in her hands,
A glass snake.

By the door,
A toy filled with rain,
A black and empty boot.

Sounds the color of sounds,
Good-bye blue and
Never-never green.

ROBIN AND THE DEAD BIRD

In the spring
Robin kneels
to hold the bird,

Dead in her hand,
wings open,
eyes absent.

In the spring
she draws, the memory
still in her hand.

ONE WAY OF LOOKING AT A BLACK-HAIRED WOMAN

Acutely hot,
Acutely forgotten,
the bank doesn't even send me statements anymore.

As my present love crumples
the air mail letter from her lover in France
and looks sad,
      triste,
he is such a bastard
      I am such a bastard,
we are all such bastards.

My roommate's pretending to be asleep,
looking with one eye to see
if I'll steal his aspirin again,
and the voyeur girls from across the way
wait breathlessly for me to expose myself
or commit suicide,
      triste,
I dissapoint them
      I am such a bastard,
we are all such bastards.

METAPHOR

If your mystery allowed me
a single metaphor tonight
do you think I'd have
the strength to take it?

As you sit at the bar, your face
a portrait framed in the space
between heads and words,

You look up at me and then away,
giving the dark silence of your eyes
to someone else tonight,

And who cares? With the juke-box
playing *Bitch* and somebody
buying Bloody Marys
a metaphor somehow seems enough.

EVENING OF RAIN

                              on one day
in January
The dull light of windows augurs infidelity
by the simple absence of a car,

No less the light of mirrors show
nothing less than nothing,
not handsome, nor striking
not special at all.

Returning in the rain
to find the car returned,
no headlight glimmer,
bodiless as it is, and no less slow
than when he drives with you,
and perhaps even slower.

The back seat whispers
and the mirror, looking back,
can do nothing but agree.

Returned to this, from light to dark,
from warmth to rain, I laugh,
you have no choice, I understand.

WHAT THE BLIND GIRL SAID

1.) At one time I had normal vision. I had sight that was 20/400, which means that what you can see at twenty feet looked like it was four hundred feet away to me. But because of my retinas, I had to face total blindness by the time I was fourteen. At first it was rough. But then I tried to tell myself, "Hey. You're going to go blind. You will have no sight. You'd better get ready." So I did.

2.) I lived in Minneapolis until my Mom and Dad split up. My Mom moved to Florida and my Dad went back to Dayton. He also fell in love there, so we stayed. But then my Step-Mom was killed in a car accident.

3.) I got my spine screwed up in the accident. My sister had the vertebrae dislocated from her neck. It was a terrible accident.

4.) After the accident we weren't allowed to go to church because Dad kind of blamed God for it. But then, after almost ten years of never going into a church, one Sunday six months ago he went. Boy was that a shock to the family.

5.) My best friend was born with cancer. He had it in his head, so they had to remove his eyeballs. He wears sunglasses all the time.

6.) I can't wait to play the drum again. I'm a drummer with the band at the Blind School. I also sing in the Glee Club, which isn't very good because I have a cold now. I'll be very rusty on the drums. But I love music; Gospel, Blues, Folk and Rock. My hero is Stevie Wonder. I figure if he can do it, so can I.

7.) I get bad coughs because I had an upper lung infection two years ago. They had to put me in the hospital. The Director of the Blind School came to me and said "I hope the Good Lord decides to heal you." I said "I hope he does too, because I want to get out of this bed." He got a real laugh from that. Keep 'em laughing, I say.

8.) My other best friend disappointed me so much recently. He was busted for marijuana. I told him to stop his excessive indulgence in that area, but it didn't work and he was busted. I don't do any of that stuff myself, drugs or anything. I like life and I figure why mess it up with drugs.

9.) I am sensitive to bright lights though. Boy, I guess I go to bed every night with a splitting headache.

10.) I can't go on airplanes either, because my eyes would pop out of my head because of the pressure. I just found that out a year ago.

PREMONITION

The smell of rain
    before it's rained
    the air heavy and wet.

Under the trees/On the bench
    by the tennis court.
The memory of her brown legs
    stretching.

Her cool hand on my shoulder,
    her hair/the rain
    as it falls.

That I might/That I might
    have her.
A soft woman/A hard woman
    a beautiful woman.

The smell of rain
    after it's rained
    the air so close and smooth.

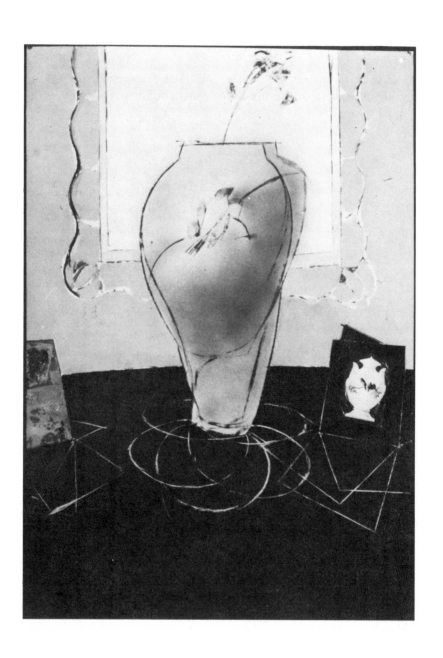

Margaret Hasse

LIGHT IN THE HEAD

for Lynn Lohr

At thirteen, she begins having fainting spells.
All indoor places are suspect,
especially churches.
The voice of the minister calls a blush
from the pale lengths of her arms.
He is reading from St. Paul, and badly.

Her imperturbable mother tongues
the backsides of her teeth.
She knows the signs.
She is glad for an excuse to remember
how sparks once flew
from the touch of everything.

Morning, and the world looks brand-new
as if all its windows had been washed.
The girl rises nimbly and steps
into her body.
She has decided to wear it
for the rest of her life.

LINGUISTICS

I wake you in the middle of the night asking you
the meaning of the word in my dream. We often ask
each other vocabulary words and we have a dictionary,
red, heavy, always open somewhere in the house. Five
paperback dictionaries, smaller, brief in their
descriptions and histories, are placed by the bed, near
the kitchen, in the car, in my study, down in the basement.

Never before at night, at 3 a.m., have I approached you
with the complexity of the dream language and half-asleep
yourself you say: "The beast . . . the big . . ." And now I
am awake enough to wonder that I asked the word,
"behemoth," and that you knew the word, "behemoth,"
and answered.

You, the answering, precise one.
Me, the one who dreamed beyond what I know.

HEAT LIGHTNING

All spring we have been waiting for rain.

In the sweat shops of the sheets
our bodies curl like drought grubs.
The commas of our shapes
punctuate the dusty distances
between what we hope for and can have.

Our nights must evolve into more
than bad dreams of heat.

Farmers' spittle sows the fields.
Bread cannot rise out of brown nurseries.
Dry land does not confess its green.

Cracked terracotta, our lips
are unsealed by need and we speak.

It is very late.
From the dark, thunder confirms
the unknown others.

NIGHT GAME AT PARADE STADIUM

—for Jim Moore

You bump into a friend in the bleachers.
He's walked out on a bad play
to sit in a second-rate field
watching the P.O. men beat the "Finks,"
a police team. It's that kind of night.

The professional ball players get power
from their buttocks.
Even those city league players of softball
have enormous hams.
The lights coat each man
with a perfection you could live with.

If you spent all night in the park,
the pleasure of the wind would overcome
exhaustion. Or you could sleep
in the field of long grass
like a lost ball,
a home run.

When the game's over and the lights cut,
you think you see the shiny back of a coin.
It's the deceit of Saran from a cigarette package
catching the stars in its sheer wrap.

MATINS OF THE BIRDS

I stand in the dark chamber
of my house, smell the
heady rot of hyacinths.
They are burning blossom white,
the after-moons of the flash photo.
Still and menacing flowers,
they encroach on the glass boundary
of my angers.

March is tired and grey-hooded.
Even the trees are enemies.
My eyes glaze over as if iced.

Women half my age are holding babies
to the sugar of their breasts.
Summer will see them on park benches
or at K-mart, tugging along a raised hand
and a small live bundle beneath.

I raise my hand to ask the questions,
I raise my hand to my eyes,
I put my hand in my lap.

Oh, amazed breath that gains its substance
from the cool air,
I can wait for the birds.
I will promise them seeds,
heated baths.
Little kings and queens of the southern court,
grace me with your return,
arrows to the heart.

Susan Hauser

HOW, LIKE THE SPRING, SLOWLY

How, like this spring, slowly
I rise from the long steel winter.

Today driving past
the funeral home,

I saw myself walking
in that door. And I remembered

I did not dress you.
I am sorry for that.

I was glad
when you were born

to bare your torso,
feel each foot

and hand, to touch
your pouch,

to bring your wet mouth
to the river of my breast.

I told the man
I wanted to dress you.

He said no. I did not argue,
did not want to feel

your skin turned to stone,
to bone,

to not bend

in the water of my arms.
Like the spring slowly
I rise from the long steel winter.

In my dreams you are often
lost. In these words I
dress you now,
sweet Aaron,

your wildflower face,
these word-wings from my fingers
folding around
your willow bones.

Slow as spring,
the spirit-milk rises.

Bring your wet mouth.

NIGHT CLASS: PETIT POINT

for Nancy

We are old in this room,
as flaky as the radiator,
and a girl's voice that
bends down the hall
and turns in to us
is too loud
for my purpose.
I get up and shut the door.
I have learned to be quiet,
but that poltergeist,
that girl I cannot see
down the high
school hall
and around that corner,
worries me.

She is talking with
a friend, and I begin
to think about you.
Night kneels against
the black mouths of these
windows, and
the woman I see there
is supposed to be me.

I look away, but
I remember the petit point
you sent me,
an original design,
immaculate stitches
on white linen,
the frayed frame held
with a machine-drawn line.
I thought then
"this is so like you,
the delicate details,
the weight
of the linen."

I turn again to the windows,
and try to imagine you
standing near me.
The faces of twelve
women and men
knock against
the brittle pains.

Turning to them:
point
by point:
I explain,
I explain.

THIS HOUSE TO CARRY

This morning
my kitchen window
is frosted
full. The sun
gleams on the imaginary
scene there—I see
a hill,
skiers,
children at a pond, frozen.

It could be though,
if my religion were different,
that those turrets of ice
are minarets,
and the bodies
I draw there
might bow
in prayer to the East.

If my religion were different,
the small chickadees
in their morning chant
at the window feeder
might speak a language
I could understand.

Chickadees.
Naming themselves
every time they open
their mouths.

Today I can only see
their shadows.
Between the sun
and the brilliant frost,
they are like the moon,
bright
on one side only,
and their dark sides

carry over
a shadow,
play on the screen
of my kitchen window.

My body joins the drama
when I stand leaping
from wall to wall,
as though afraid
of the voices
from the flocks
outside.

I go to another window.
Here chance has left
an eye space
I can peer through.

It is like wearing
a chador,
the black cloth
of these rooms
folded around me,

and I pretending
I am not
inside.

How slowly I move
with this house to carry!

HAIR COMBING

Long, my hair falls
past the middle
of my back.

You ask to comb it.
Your own hair,
young,
is too easy for you.
You want
your fingers tangled
in this woman's mane.

I am so strong!
If you can comb this hair,
you, too, will be
a woman.

You have watched me
mornings, one hand
turning the glory knot,

the other
locking it in place.

Have watched me then
enter the day
and return at night

to spill the dark
brown waterfall
into your lap.

It looks easy,
this raising and lowering
of hair,
as though it were a flag

and I a country.
You do not know

I am well defended.
In sleep
I guard against
the dream troops,
and by day
my eyes, quick
and brown with night,
stop every movement.

I have kept this from you.

Tonight
you ask again.
Stand beside me.
Woman.
Youth.
In your flat body,
fingers humming, open
to the polishing stone.

I let you take the pins out.

You comb and comb.
Every time the knot slips your hold.

I do not help.

You are embarrassed.
And hurt.

And it is true.
I have done this to you.

FOUR LADIES SLEEPING/FIVE

after I came along, caught
too by the storm
that turned this airport
into port.

In the women's lounge
I stir my coat, my bag,
my bundles
into a circle
in which I will drowse.

The other women, already moored,
sleep headless,
each with a turban
of sweater or scarf,
bringing dark
through their eyes
to their bodies.

I can hear them breathe.
Can hear through the door
voices and machines.
Can hear
in a small room off this one
a gurney squek in and then out,
slipping off into the snow-shroud
with another woman.

How did she come to be lost?

I hold my wallet and ticket
tighter against my stomach,
press to my heart
the little cylinder of pills
that keep peace there,

tug on the rope
I have threaded through
the handles of my baggage.

Other women go by.
They look into this room
each pile
with its own heartbeat,
full of heaped clothing,
each pile
with its own heartbeat,
its own dream, each
with a ticket
and a time.

Each safe-bound
she thinks
by sex

and by the light
that pours down on us.

EACH DAY NOW

I ski, the satin arms
of the track
drawing me
out to the field.

There the weeds
write   in pencil
thin shadows: goldenrod,
and milkweed;
and this
is silvery conquefoil;
in summer
its small yellow flowers
rub like coins
in the pocket
of the sun.

Even now
the brittle bells
seem to talk; and they
are stubborn: all
this winter wind has not shaken
them loose.

Overhead
a scarf of grosbeaks
folds
onto the shoulders
of those trees,
and ahead
a Pileated Woodpecker:

KA KA KA KA KA!

I, too, can
call names.
I thrust yours
into the air.
It goes away,
and it comes back.

Watching the sky,
I see the damn clouds
skipping.

I throw your name again;
and once again.

Three times.
That is enough
for a beginner.

Martha Roth

A WAITRESS JOURNAL

Week 1.—The first two days, they had me work singles and deuces, in a safe place, right by the serving counter, the bar, the coffeemaker. Thursday I had four tables; Friday, five. The next Monday I had six tables.

"You don't look like a waitress," said a man on the second day. He was eating alone, drinking Manhattans on the rocks and picking his teeth with a matchbook cover.

"Well, I'm new."

"No, now I didn't mean you weren't a good waitress. I just meant, you don't look like the others."

I went hot with sudden, murderous anger, but I swallowed it and smiled. He had curly, graying fair hair. "Good luck in the job," he said softly, when he left. A dollar lay on the table; my first bill.

Week 2.—It's not old ladies who are bad tippers, and it's not young people, or black people. It's bad people: people who feel bad about themselves, hostile, tightly wound, false. Ugly people who eat alone, late. Selfish people. A few women I come to know, regulars; they eat in the Grill every day, without tipping. How do they dare?

The soups have begun to repeat: chicken noodle, chicken and rice, beef and barley, beef and vegetable, split pea, navy bean, tomato. On Fridays we have clam chowder, the New England style with milk and big chunks of potato.

The entrees repeat, too: hot bratwurst, spinach salad, Salisbury steak. I'm learning the menu, learning to ask what dressing they want on their salad, when they order a dish that comes with a salad. I'm learning about potato *or* vegetable and potato *and* vegetable, what gets cole slaw, when to bring a roll.

Our most popular lunch is the soup and sandwich combination: $3.60 for a cup of soup and a "bountiful sandwich of egg salad, tuna salad, ham salad, liverwurst, or thuringer on white, whole wheat, or pumpernickel rye," with a beverage and a small sundae.

I hear the others calling the sundae a "BL." "That's 'cause the soup-and-sandwich useda be a businessman's lunch, BL, so we still call it that," Sophie tells me over her shoulder.

The soup comes in a white cup that I have to take out of the top drawer of a warming cabinet and fill from an electric soup tureen. Often the china is hot enough to hurt my fingers even before I fill it with hot soup. I place the cup on a plate between fanned-out halves of the sandwich, when Marlene the sandwich girl puts it up; add a soup spoon and a cellophane package of crackers and serve the plate lunch. Some of us put the soup cup on a saucer, but it's faster if we don't. The sandwich comes with a single carrot curl and two ribbed pickle slices, the kind of pickles that set your teeth against one another.

Some of the waitresses put a sprig of parsley on the soup-and-sandwich, but they are people who would put parsley on hot fudge. Once, when they ran out of pickles, Leona the stand-in sandwich girl with hairy arms substituted chunks of cantaloupe. But that was later, in the fourth week.

We are all girls, except of course Tommy the grill cook and Glenn the bartender. Glenn's eyes cross violently, and he has a sour temper. I wonder what the world looks like, to him. In these early weeks I try to ingratiate myself. I smile a lot and thank all the cooks by name—Arlene the salad girl, Marlene the regular sandwich girl, Leona, Trudy the steam table girl, Zona the dessert girl. And Glenn and Tommy. When I make a mistake, I apologize and say, "Some day I'll learn."

When one of them makes a mistake, I do the same, figuring that it is my unfamiliar style that has caused the mistake. We will learn to fit. If I say to Arlene, "Small tossed salad with oil and vinegar," she does not hear me. She'll hear me when I learn to say, "Salad Italian," and "Salad thousand."

Arlene and Marlene and the men are thin. Zona is fat; Trudy is wider than she is high. Leona and the other waitresses are big busty women, except for a blonde named Karen. I have never seen Karen eat anything unfried or drink anything uncola, and she must weight 105 pounds soaking wet.

The dish-room people are retarded. Leon, the chief, has tongue-tie and is a toucher. He is the only toucher, and he has a bad temper. No one can understand what he says, whether he is pissed off or not. It took him a while to learn my name. "Mossa," he calls me, like a little child. He is very strong. When we run out of ice, he lugs the tub of fresh ice chips down from the sixth-floor ice machine and empties it into the sink, where we can shovel it into water pitchers, iced tea, and soft drinks.

One of the dish-room people is a silent black woman in a hairnet. She looks distressed all of the time but says nothing.

Week 3.—On Friday, when I went to pick up my paycheck, I found that they had not got me on the computer. I'll have to wait another week to get paid. "You can get a cash advance, though," the cashier tells me. "Go talk to Lynn Peterson."

Lynn Peterson is Director of Personnel for the whole store. She gives me a fishy eye and a pearly smile. "Sure, Martha. All you have to do is sign against your advance. I'll give you a voucher for cash, then go to the check-cashing window, not the cashier, and she'll give you the money. Okay?"

"Okay." I had to queue to see her; I have to queue again to get the money. I feel angry and humiliated.

By Monday, I have come down with a really bad cold, my first in years. It accompanied my period. I stuff a bar napkin into one of my deep pockets and blow my nose when my back is turned to the customers.

I worked dinner on Monday. My nice, tired, harried supervisor Sophie asked me to; the one scheduled to work had "let her down." I am putty in Sophie's hands. She does everything at high speed and she says things like, "You have these six tables, two, two, and two, and then those three over there," but she never loses her temper and she always answers questions, even though the answers are sometimes less than useful.

They have stopped floating me. I have a regular station, now. I took two stations at dinner on Monday. It was fun. At dinner, people drink more, spend more, tip more. We bring them a little plate of Ritz crackers and cheese spread with their drinks.

Baked potatoes are available at dinner, along with "whipped" and French fried. The "whipped" is mixed from a powder of dried potatoes, food starch, and anti-oxidants, and looks exhausted, as in "I'm whipped." I think the French fries are real potatoes, but I don't know for sure; they come frozen. I do know that McDonald's has perfected a potato-based mixture that can be extruded into uniform shapes and deep-fried, and the technique has caught on in the food business. Many places sell something like it as "French fries."

So far as I know, it isn't possible to fake a baked potato, although my mother will tell you that they're not really *baked*, they wrap them in tinfoil and that way, of course, what you get is a *steamed* potato, as in "I'm really steamed."

By the middle of the third week I have learned to go straight into the dish room to fetch the deep trays of silverware. I lug them into the dining room, then go back for trays of coffee mugs, water glasses, and ashtrays. One morning, Leon feels affectionate. He is patting waitresses' hair and kissing them on the cheek. Maxine winces as he pulls her to him. "Good Lee," she says, distractedly.

"Nice Lee," says Jean, when he hugs her.

The next time I cross in front of him, he lunges for me. "No, Lee, not today. I just don't want to be touched."

"Hickum, Mossa, hoo-woo."

"*No*." I turn away.

The crease between his brows deepens. "Fuckin bitch! Hossoo, Mossa, bitch! Hoo-woo, hoo-woo!" He stumps into the dish room and throws something metal on the cement floor. "Hoo fa doo, woo fa, mossoo," clang, clang, "hammy goko dowoofa! Bitch! Mossa doo goko, ha gummy hoo!" Something ceramic is thrown, and breaks.

Lena bustles after him, "Lee! Stop it! Not everyone wants a kiss! You have to learn to take no for an answer!"

"Sup up!" he rages at her.

"Don't you tell *me* to shut up," she booms.

"Suh-up, suh-up, sowy bitch, suh-up, swee—"

"Le-*on!*" She marches in after him.

"She should get Glenn," mutters Maxine. "He minds Glenn."

We have to set our tables, tear up our parsley, write the date in our books of customer checks. I'm a little shaken, but the next time I see Leon he acts as though nothing happened. "Hoo, Mossa, hi you?"

On Friday, I utterly lost it—my concentration, composure, memory. A lot of people sat down all at once. I had two or three tables of all men. I took their orders and promptly forgot that I had ever seen them before. I rushed about, fetching drinks, taking new orders. My customers grew restive; they expect me to bring them things. But what?

Grilled ham and cheese grow cold on the serving counter. I confuse Coke and Tab. I bring the easy orders, like club sandwiches, and let the difficult ones sit. I fight panic, my heart thumping like a dog's hind leg. I forget tea; I forget milk; I don't bring straws or lemon or salad dressing with the taco salads. It takes me a long time to write out the checks. A hot mist creeps around the frame of my vision.

I write out the checks slowly, pettifogging over tax tables while gravy congeals on the fricasseed chicken and the French dip loses heart. I pore over my book, desperate for evidence. Who ordered what? Who are these people, what do they want? Skinny Karen and Yolande, the nice waitress who wears a jeweled name tag, don't even write down their orders until they make out the checks. They must belong to a different species. All the good parsley is gone; the cheese has toughened on the cheeseburgers.

I am moving as fast as I can, but the hot mist in my head dissolves memory. I come out of the pantry, a black-and-white BL in each hand, and I see the irritated frown on a customer's face. Only then do I remember that he ordered Sprite, and someone else at that table ordered iced tea. So I plop the sundaes down gracelessly and sprint back fifty yards for the drinks. On my way to the table, I grab a tray and pile the cheeseburgers on, as though they had just come up. But I forget the ketchup. And this one wants mustard, too.

Monday, Oct. 26.—My skirt always clings on Mondays, because I wash and dry the uniform over the weekend, and my stockings are clean. June gives me a can of anti-static spray and makes me go into a utility closet and spray my lower limbs in darkness. I come out smelling peculiar and my skirt still rides up. "A little more around your knees, dear," says June.

I eat with the others, at 2:00. They all smoke. Dear Yoly holds her cigarette and fork in the same hand. Today is the first day back for a white-haired waitress named Liane who has had a lung removed, with a malignant tumor in it. She looks exhausted. "Tired, Leenie?"

"I'm OK. I'll be all right."

"It'll take a while," says Minnie, adjusting her wig. "Look at me, I was just down with a virus for three months, but I'm still not right yet."

Liane grins. "Yeah, but you're old."

Glenn the bartender talks about his little son, who lives with his divorced wife but visits frequently. "He likes to sit in the bathtub after the water gets cold, but I won't let him; I don't want him to catch cold. So I let the water out. But he sticks his toe in the drain, so the water won't go out. Last night I says, 'Watch out! It'll get you, toe and all!' But he says, 'No it won't, Daddy. Look, my toe comes back!' "

"Ah-ha," says Yoly. "My toe comes back."

"Can you beat that?" Glenn marvels. "I don't know where he gets it."

"Smart kid."

My last customer today is a young blond man who sits down and counts his money. "What kind of wine you have?" he asks me, smoothing out dollar bills.

"Chablis, Burgundy, and rosé. They're all California."

"Burgundy's red, right? OK, gimme a glass of Burgundy." His blue eyes are wet.

"A glass costs a dollar, but a two-glass carafe is only a dollar-fifty."

"I'm going to have more'n two glasses, but I might as well start with a craft. Bring me a craft."

"Would you like to order lunch now, or wait?"

"This is all I'm going to have."

"Are you sure?" I'm taking responsibility for him.

"Oh, yes."

"Glenn, he just wants to order wine, says he's not going to eat."

"What is he, drunk?"

"Well, no."

Glenn shrugs. "There's nothing wrong with that." So I bring the Burgundy, and he smokes, and drinks it, and orders another. His face droops lower and lower over the table. He is still smoking while I clean up, wiping the counters, washing tabletops, setting out mats and napkins for tomorrow.

Monday, Dec. 14.—Over the weekend I dreamed of meat; I dreamed of waitressing. Split pea and beef noodle soup. This is the last day for the prime rib. In my dream, I believe I am the meat.

There is a regular customer we call the Manhattan Lady; she always comes about 11:10, and she always sits at the same table, and she wears the same hat and coat all winter. From a distance she is merely eccentric, but close to, one sees she is very old, very dirty, and very mad.

Ladybug throws a fit. "Shit! I don't want to cook that stuff no more! I'm *tired* of cooking that food!"

"I know just what you mean," says Sharon, her hands busy. "Whooo!"

We have a new waitress, thin and pocked, with dry blonde hair and sooty eyes: Kim. My station this week is a long strip down the side of the dining-room: eight deuces, two squares, and one of the big rounds. Kim spends her first hour or two looking on and laughing hectically if I catch her eye.

About 11:45 we are having trouble with the coffeemaker. I try to ease out the top piece to see whether it has been turned on, and the machine spatters me with boiling water, scalding my hand. I spend much of the next two hours plunging it into ice water.

Gail and Sharon leap to take care of me. "Are you all right?"

"Ice! Ice! Put it on ice!"

"You should report it."

"Go down to Personnel."

"Is it red?"

"It's pretty red, you better report it."

"Keep it in the cold."

"Go down to Personnel."

"You better tell Joan."

"You OK?"

"Drink! You should drink! Drink plenty! Replace the fluids!"

"I'll be OK." It does hurt like the devil if I take it out of the ice water for long; also, I'm mildly shocked, and trembling. My customers clamor for coffee, but the one machine isn't working, so we limp along with a half-supply.

When most of the customers are gone, I let Sharon persuade me to go to Personnel, where a very young clerk writes down the date, my employee number, and the nature of the injury. She gives me a tube of ointment and a gauze pad. The scald hurts. "I'm pissed," I tell her, "and I want to complain."

She tells me to complain first to Lena.

Back upstairs, everyone clucks over my gauzed, anointed hand. I complain to Lena.

"What do you mean, you want to complain?" she barks. "It was your own fault."

"Well, I know I shouldn't have tried to slide out the drip top—"

"You're right, you shouldn't. Don't ever—"

"But that little wire cage that holds the full filter in, when you pour the coffee grounds into it?—that was missing. Somebody tossed it into the rubbish."

"You mean the garbage."

"Yes, when they threw out the used filter, you know how we do. That's why the machine was acting funny, because that wire cage was gone."

"Well, I'm very sorry about your hand," she says, standing up and looking past me, "but there's nothing wrong with that machine. We used it all day yesterday. Now you know not to do that any more. If something's wrong with the machine, turn it off and come and get me. I'm around, you know."

I nod and agree, but later I start a slow, Oliver Hardy sort of burn. Nobody ever showed me how the fucking coffeemaker works. I don't even drink coffee. And, for Christ's sake, the bland instruction to turn off the machine—of course, that's what the boss will say. Of course, it's what one should do, according to OSHA. But at 11:45, with the dining room filling up fast and everyone waiting for coffee—some cookbook writer calls it "the Midwestern apéritif"—waitresses will try to fix a coffeemaker themselves, before they'll turn it off and drop the rhythm of work to go find the supervisor.

I have a friend who used to be married to a big handsome man who built nuclear power plants. She told me about his anger at the men on his crew who wouldn't use the decontamination procedures. "He says it's just macho," she told me. "They think it's tough not to wear the lead-lined gloves, even." We agreed, horrified, that the root of the evil was machismo—"Testosterone poisoning," she said, with a bitter laugh.

But now I find myself wondering whether safety precautions are always made into a double bind for workers. Does putting on the gloves mean that they clock fewer minutes on the job? Are they paid for productivity, and does decontamination eat into their time?

Lauren, the lanky downstairs busboy, is a natural foods freak. He eats enormous salads and sandwiches entirely covered with alfalfa sprouts. Today he addressed his first spontaneous utterance to me: "You know what's best for burns? Put Vitamin E on it."

I nod.

"You mean, rub it on?" asks Lana, with a greedy shudder.

"Yes," I say, "you open up a cap and pour the oil right onto the burned skin."

"That's right," says Lauren.

"No wonder I get zits from that stuff," she says, and laughs.

Thursday, Dec. 24.—Christmas Eve. The Minnesota Room is closed; we work in the Grill. Business is slow, so slow that little Betty Bear starts saying at about noon, "I heard we're going to close early."

"Don't listen to Betty," say Yoly and Maxine. "She don't know what she's talkin' about."

Sophie is hostess. I've never seen her out of uniform; she is handsome and very hostessy in a pink and green suit. She carries with her a flat piece of cracker-bread, and before the restaurant opens she forms us into a circle. "I'm going to wish you the way we do on Christmas Eve. This is a Polish custom. We break bread with each other. Long life and health to you in 1982. That's the way we do. Now you take a piece." She says it to each of us in turn, but before the circle is complete, the first customers have come in.

Later, she catches me at the coffee machine. "Now, I'm going to show you an old Polish custom. Good health and good future in the coming year. Now, take a piece."

"Thank you, Sophie, and the same to you." I kiss her powdered cheek. "It's matzoh, Sophie," I called after her, but it's more like fish food.

Soups are tomato-rice and navy bean. I'm sent to Mud Lake, but it's all right—we aren't very busy, and I manage the long trips back to the counter, the pantry, or the dish room better than the last time. A party of six sits at my corner table, three young couples. One of the men has his jaws wired, like Al Pacino in *The Godfather*; he orders strained tomato soup and a wild cherry malt.

"Oh god," I gibber in the pantry, "do we have a strainer? Anybody have a sieve? A strainer?"

"I got a strainer upstairs," says Fred, finally, hurling himself up the spiral stairs. He always hates to cook down here in the Grill; the others are glum or stupid and don't laugh at him the way we do upstairs.

He comes down with an old, bent strainer, and I feel bonded to him, family. I ladle the tomato soup carefully through the sieve, sans rice, and deliver it with a straw. Zona makes my customer a beautifully thinned malt.

All through the shift I hear Sophie giving her traditional Polish rap to her steady customers, breaking off bits of the wafer. Sometimes she says a couple of words in Polish. I hum *In dulce jubilo* and wish my customers a merry Christmas. When you're in the mood, waitressing is like giving a lunch party every day; twenty lunch parties every day.

Mary Virginia Micka

LETTER TO MY LANDLADY

Dear, dear Eva,
                In your house everything
works: hot runs hot and cold runs
cold and what needs to go down goes directly
down—you never hesitate. You told me
there's nothing much up here, but
what about these windows? I count
fourteen; all of them open, close and
lock and the screens slide up and down on
fourteen different views of trees, roofs with
chimneys smoking, paths criss-crossing
to school, Mary Ann's fence and clothespin
bag and at 1:15 the mailman's cap
turning. The bed accommodates me like
the countryside this village sleeps in, as do
twenty-nine hooks per closet—every room
has its big closet. And I cannot believe
your smooth-springing ironing board.
                                 True,

your knives are what you said, dull, but I see
you laugh through what you can't cut. Nor
do the cups match any of the saucers. Yet, vision-
imbalanced myself, I stand to admire
your various resources, like the one mirror
giving me only the top half and the other,
the other—well, the full picture of me
lording around your abundant house, that's
more than you could take in all at once
anyway. So here's the rent again.

SMALL THINGS TELL US

Oh, the cats in this town have their secrets.
They know: 1) about Scamper, missing
since August, long and lean like
a panther—well, too bad for Judy with
all her rewards; and 2) about Gracie
and Boots on their way back
to Sullivan Street without telling; Gracie's also
this minute, if only you knew, simmering
in fine calico on a certain porch
in the village; and 3) about dogs like
that fool of an overgrown schnauzer who
finds his way out through the upstairs
window, all right, but then yelps
on the ledge for help down—he can't handle
his freedom; that mustard-colored police
is a violent brute; the retriever uses her tail
like an oar but is harmless enough; and 4)
pay no attention to mutts.
                Every cat in town
knows at least the above, besides where's
the fire the trucks go screaming out after and—
what is suspected perhaps by the hostess, if
not by her famished guest—that the pizza
while still lowly and raw was stepped into, then
out of, and the sauce licked by someone
not saying.
              Finally, a very few cats have been
baptized into the mysteries. This explains
Lily, who streaks through the iris and
half an hour later streaks back; this sustains
Avatar's view walking his fence that
in these gardens, clearly, there can be no
pardoning the beans their small blight— nor the errant
squash, for that matter: it is precisely
these small flaws you see that are so telling.

TWO VARIATIONS

1. Waking in Air

   Already this morning one house
   in the white village feels
   a scarf of orange anemones float
   down without wrinkle
   over a table in the white light.
                                    As
   these bright flowers ripple the air
   someone next door smiles
   deeper into her dream
   and does not hear
                          a third neighbor
   descending his stair, pausing
   to watch shawl upon shawl of new snow
   sinking over the field.
                            So soft this descent,
   a vast extension of sleep, he must
   blink away dark when
   at the field's far edge a lone skier,
   orange and black, leans
   into the trackless space.
                              But once he is certain
   that color is entering the air,
   then the sleeper will open her eyes.

2. Already This Morning

   Beyond my window someone
   last night dreamed me this
   field of new snow without sign
   drifting the house down deeper
   than signs into sleep long
   before morning all still
   dreaming a white drift and I here
   without sound far drifting until
   someone already other
   beside me snaps

and then settles an orange print
breakfast cloth and a skier
dark in the distance leans
into the field, taking
the trackless space.

RINSE O WHITE

When it says right here on the label
Do Not Bleach, what are you supposed to do,
for god's sake, about the spots? Beer and
salad dressing and look at all that cat
scat. What happens when you bleach them
anyway, these polyester white-to-begin-
with stretch-to-your-shape pants you were
a fool to buy in the first place? Well,
what? Do they end up yellow? rot
from the inside out? slow-burn
through the cuff or in the pockets?
If so, then better go
with the spots, start with scrub
as much as possible between
your heavy-duty no-bleach raw
knuckles, imitating the ritual of
washboards and before that beating until
clean on ancient rocks and then when
this doesn't work, simply kneel down in
maybe even the mud in pure acknowledgement
to the manufacturer that as far as his
whites are concerned, you're out
beyond your depth.

THE WEBBING

Bowls of air from your inland lake
spread a fine blue far
over my lap where loose in sunlight
your letter the color of maize
and your blown hair
catches me in the lift
of your life together—

    we spent the day
    webbing wild rice; you
    beat gently and the rice comes
    tinkling into the boat, and the mallards
    all free, and the air crisp-warm
    and so peaceful and
    we think of you, so when you can,
    write—

Two young gleaners bending
September light, stroking the rice-
rush, feeling wild wings in a blood-rush beating
such sweet kernels of harvest
I must begin
bending strand by strand gently back
into your lives against all future winters
this high light
flow of love webbing thousands of miles
crisp-warm today and so peaceful.

FOR DAYS MY STUDENT'S ABSENT

In handwriting round as any child's
you say, hoping it will be clear,
*history is a time when a lot of mistakes
are made,* and I must leave
your text to stare down
drifts and drifts of cast-off tries
the maples made this year: no wise,
crisp, multicolored ways to right
one half the error of one's life
suggest themselves. And I sigh inward, oh
my dear, what you say—nothing
was ever more true. Yet I wonder
that you know. Day after day—
your still pale face, wild eyes—you never
come where are you? Tell me. *I met this
older guy,* and I skim
p. 4, p. 5, willing
to learn *Barry can tell
who is your friend and who isn't
really,* and I nod yes, we need desperately
to know this can be done, what with our
history and all, as you say, drifting us
down toward the end, I think it is the end,
where you say, *I want badly
to begin new things now, and Barry
is my beginning,* hoping it will be clear.

FAMILY LIFE

Don't kid yourself
no one's single   owns
all these feelings
olive sprouts around the table
push and pinch
        days you'd like to get away
        to other people's
and give you enough grief   lie and sneak
or crowd you right out to the edge
and then split

quiet ones you want to watch close
not out for blood but
so sad wistful your heart aches
how you know they're even there

and at night dead tired
pile in   each one's got to be first
        me (cry)   me (laugh)   me me
        grab in lightning and thunder
how each one's going to make it

you wonder   do what you can
to watch over.

LOST UNTIL FOUND

my umbrella my bathrobe were hers

yesterday the umbrella fell away
secretly   climbing the bus
something at my arm missing
that windbreak rainbreak   well
it's time now   go on
without it

then out of dark sleep to cry
mother   o mother   see
crowds of us
deep drenched in
too soon not knowing
your shade shelter
slips all untimely no matter when
where   all of us

in our pain then   patience   listen
o mother   your soft
sleeve still cover us until
sunbreak

MY HOUSE

You come to my house the scent of warm
cinnamon drawing you in. I draw up your chair then
attend as the visit begins: you smile
through the steam of the tea and I smile but
look can you hear can you see how
under this face this arrangement
of cups I begin to take
leave am withdrawn
along the smooth floor (scrubbed
for your coming) under the door down
the steps to my cellar? My cellar lies
deeper than you might think but
there I am called to descend regardless
of guests, to where my old renters
rage without word
without form rise to engage me,
wanting to buy.

Not wanting to sell I silent want only . . .

You gathering crumbs as the visit goes on: they
draw closer to nibble then sip in my throat
come sell us your house . . .

you sipping my tea then the cinnamon stuck
to your fingers I try smiling
under your eyes reach
for your cup the tea swelling up to the brim
you sighing I shouldn't but yes . . .

I wordless to cry for your hand
no finger urgent can find sink back under
ashamed of my cellar supporting our house
in terror in pity for me and for thee . . . .

Tom Hansen

THE MAN IN THE MOON'S LOONY BROTHER

(drawing by Paul, age 7)

If you stare too long at the sun,
it starts staring back—
those sleepwalker eyes disguised as fried eggs
sunny side up and holding.
That inexplicable pig snout
aimed your way, sniffing you out.
That smile hunked out of a jack-o'-lantern.
Who could believe such a face?

At night, when no one can see him,
his yellow-white fire
splinters into a rainbow of tongue-beams
or fins.
His eggy-pig-pumpkinness
glories the gathering dark all about him.
Those blind hosannahs. That lost
language of light.

IN OLDEN DAYS

(drawing by Paul, age 7)

The cave entrance, minus cave,
balanced carefully all about him.
He, the cave man, standing there
smiling a wild toothless smile and
waving flat flippers. No one knows why.
Above him, a bird angles left—
diagonal of good luck.
Below, the vast brown body of earth.

This world of correspondences . . . .
How the cave man's mismatched flippers
repeat themselves in the bee's wings.
How redbird and greenosaur,
wearing the two great colors of life,
stare at that same vacant space—
just beyond the edge of the drawing
where something is waiting to happen.

How the bodies of all earth's children
are built of stone.
And everything—even the tree-sized flower,
even the Shiva-armed beetle—
waves at you, the viewer,
as if it knew your name
and welcomed you here.
As if, before they turned to dust, to say:

You, who move through this house,
wrapped in darkness, sleepwalking—
this dance of correspondences
is your waking.
We who are nothing but gray stone
stand here before you—wordless, unmoving.
The story we wait to tell
must be one of your making.

GOD

(drawing by Christopher, age 5)

"Those long things might be arms
that he controls people with—
He reaches down and makes you walk.
You see that kind of thing
coming out of his mouth?
I don't know what that's for,
but you see those long things going through his legs?
Those are icicles hanging down like snow
in the cave he is going in."

How clear it seems to him—
all that talk of arms and mouth and legs
where there are none.
Behind those familiar names
lies the ghost of abstraction:
a dance of spidery lines. A visible absence.
So this is nothing. No thing at all.
It is only the green ferment
of a child's imagination.

How do you know this is God?
"Because that's what I was thinking of."
What is God like?
"He is green and all stretched out,
sort of like lightning."
What does he think of alone all the time?
"He counts stars and waits for the seeds to grow."
Does he ever worry about people?
"He wants us to do things right."

In the small galaxy of a child's mind,
thoughts ignite and roar off like fireworks,
trailing sparks into the summer night.
What does God think of fireworks?
"He thinks it must be somebody's birthday."
So it is, my son. For even now,
I see the candles burning.
I see icicles hanging down like snow
in the cave he is going in.

ME

(drawing by Christopher, age 6)

Me with my halo of coiled curls
that circle my head like a wreath.
Me with my eyes like lopsided fried eggs,
my bare-bump nose, and big crooked smile.

Me with my shirt that looks like a dress
and my boots that look like black stockings.
Me with my vaguely androgynous Santa Claus look—
how I hanker to crawl down your chimney.

Me with no hands. I am safe:
nothing but stumps up these sleeves.
Me with my mismatched peg legs.
Who yearns to hobble to my hard music?

Paper-faced me, who stares at the stranger
who stares at the paper, then runs away—
waving his two good terrified hands,
and crying, "Not me! Not me!"

FACES OF THE COOK

(seven drawings by Christopher, age 4)

What does it take to scare a cook?
Another cook, ha ha.
                              —Anon.

Face One

Here is Cook, wearing his hat.
Big crooked smile aimed left.
His magic button is red
and so are all the holes in his head,
those circles so close to round.
The world is four years old today,
smiling at things we can't see.

Face Two

Something happened. We stare
and hang on to our questions.
Like why his head is squeezed out of round
and his face is an accident, waiting.
He hears it coming and holds his breath.
A year passes. He exhales.
This continues all night.

Face Three

Cook is white as any cliché.
Something nameless he sees.
Himself? His shadow walking away? His reflection
rising out of the mirror, red and burning
and naming names and his the first on the list?
Or is it as white as he is—the thing out there?
Cook, what is it you cannot bear to bear?

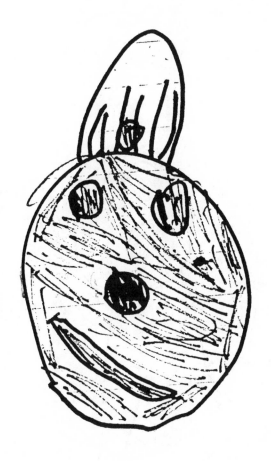

Face Four

This is the story of water.
There is a sky inside his head:
a bucket of rain, a drowning,
somebody dying of thirst.
Cook is cold. It is night. There is no one.
If he had hands, he could teach them
to pray to each other.

Face Five

His hat is gone. He is saved. So it seems.
Cruciform stars lie about him.
Crippled emblems and dreams
of the body's ascension.
This is Cook, this falling-to-earth,
this all-head-and-legs walking air.
With stars,
without the chance of a ghost.
No way to get out of there.

Face Six

His legs are gone. He has run out of air.
Below him the water is blue, streaked green.
It stands at attention, licking, waiting,
aching to hold his body.
The eight remaining stars are healed—
they are more nearly crosses now.
They are luminous and removed
and without meaning.

It is no use turning the paper flat
and staring down the length of it.
There is no secret message. Nothing.
This is a four-year-old drawing
of air and water and fire.
See how Cook's face burns.
See the hungry water standing on tiptoe.

Cook, stranger, somebody's brother,
Jesus marooned on the water—
your story is all but over.
Tell it and drown.

Face Seven

Cook is locked in a block of ice
submerged in orange liquid.
His hat is a lumberjack's hat
with a hole in the front.
Off to the left
the sticky, smoldering
orange-juice fires of hell
squeeze into his cell.

Christopher asks about the mouth.
He can't remember drawing it.
The answer is: "Only Cook knows."
The answer is: "Cook never tells."

4:00 a.m. Someone is up.
Under the glow of fluorescent tubes,
the room is a pale cube
floating through darkness.
6:00 a.m. The sky turns orange and runny.
It leaks through the window.
All the lumberjacks in the world
poke holes in their hats with blind fingers.
Their mouths cave in.
The congress of spiders convenes.

Margot Fortunato Kriel

HER LETTER TO A PATRON, NAPLES 1649

Since you ask the price
of my figures, I will tell you,
Signore: one hundred *scudi* per figure
or you will not possess
a canvas by Artemisia.
My painted flesh will never crack
like Anguissola's. She clothed
herself in reticent colors.
My Judith's strong arm
ends in a sword.

In each canvas, I battle
with light and shade, so
at nineteen I was taught
by the man my father hired.
His hand guided mine
as we painted callas,
their red heads hissing
with sun. We entered the clash
of ash and flame until
as I commanded surrender,
he broke the brush
from my hand, tore
the clothes from my breast,
and forced me to the ground.
Thumbscrew at my nail,
I was accused of inviting rape,
but I defended only my virtue
lost in a fallen brush.

Now I paint Judith.
Unarmed, she walked
into the tent of Holofernes.
With only a candle,

she made him drunk
with ease and certainty.
I have beheaded many men.

Each canvas a study
in brocade and blood,
my maid holds the fruit
of the general's head
while I, with sword
and candle, listen
for the approach of fame.

You ask for a madonna.
My madonnas are few.
Signore, the soul of Caesar
lives in this woman.
Mary means nothing to me.
My painter's strong arm
ends in a sword.

*The biographical details come from letters and biographies of the Italian
baroque painter, Artemisia Gentileschi. She painted many versions of the
biblical heroine Judith.

WALKING THE BEACH

When you walked away from us
down the beach, sometimes
I kept up with you
as the wind cleared your face
of any resemblance
to the mother I knew.

Wanting to call, I was
afraid that your eyes
would turn to shells,
your mouth to a whisper.

On you steered,
pelican skimming heavy-bodied
close to the waves,
as I let you go, amazed
at you who awkwardly
fed us close to your face
and set us so freely away.

WINTER MOOD

After a week of snow,
windshields clogged with salt,
the woodpile next door stares with eyes
cut from summer's trees. My love,
it is a time for courage and the slow heart.

On the kitchen table, a jar of basil
reminds me of summer when distance
announced its sweetness through long evenings
and what we did not know entered
the morning mind. Now the only illusion
is your blue-shirted arm reflected
in a window darkened into mirror.

At times we have little to say
or else words fly to leave us cold.
Surely we can blame the season,
but in the quiet, the slow descent
of what may happen
weights us to the ground.

THE TOUCH

He was the boy who touched
women's clothes, combed his mother's hair.
He sat close to the TV
when women in slips lifted
their arms, his fingers played in silk.
The family was afraid of him,
too often with women;
his lips on sleeves, he lingered
with girls who laughed and talked.
He should learn to be with men.

Later in rice paddies
he stabbed an Asian,
he could not tell if it
was man or woman. The falling head
rested in his hand, the hair
an old remembered comfort.

Home in Pittsburgh, he watched women
in bars, the light on their knees,
hair waving gently down their backs.
Sometimes he touched himself.

He married a large woman
but soon was lost,
had a child he could not bear
to touch, and often begged silently
to be let out. His wife
caressed him, but next to her,
he became a small boy
who could not touch her hair
waving gently above his trembling, upraised hands.

WALKING BY THE WALL

Strong-legged daughter of ten,
you went reluctant with me
along the river road. What need
had you for exercise?
I was the one, when you
were smaller than one day's cry,
felt I must pull you into being.
Now you weight my arm.
Wooing, I tell you
the golden lilies close at night,
and picking one, you say,
"Day-lilies, I know."

Above the freeway,
you run your hand along
the wall, concrete slabs
that alternate rough
and smooth. You call,
"The rough is cooler
than the smooth." It's your game
I play, putting my hands
against the slabs. I don't want
to tell you that the sun,
which glows and sinks behind
the wall, makes neither warmer
to my touch. So wooing you,
I give a reason. "The rough,
with more ridges, cools.
The smooth keeps the heat it holds."
You walk ahead, drop
the lily and turn
to tell me, "Mother,
you always know,
you never let me wonder."

PROUST AT LAKE MICHIGAN

for Chris Flagler

I.

Jogging is good for the health.
Chris, you lead the way. I follow,
short of breath, clutching my coat.
Two miles down, the atomic plant
breathes clouds of steam.

We splash through bone-chilling water, around bricks and carcasses of
huge fish as well as the alewives. They shine silver, soft underfoot. We
climb huge sand dunes separated by a valley with its own vegetation.
At the top, we survey the hazy water and talk about our motherhood.
You rocked my daughter when she could not sleep. Your mother died
when your son was born. In each of your children, you look for her,
but there is no resemblance.

Later I sit on a rug next
to the fire while you,
with broom and stick,
clean the beach. You tell me,
"My mother tore old clothes
into rags to make those rugs.
Now we walk over her shawl,
plaid skirts, an old cape,
and our own abundant accident."

II.

As a child, I could expect, when we went to the beach, that my father
would never sit on the sand. Gathered around his waist, on a cord tied
in a long loop, his brown trunks waved gently around his legs.
Standing on the blanket, he ate hard-cooked eggs. Then he cast into
the surf and reeled in the line. When we returned to the car, he cleaned
my feet with a brown whisk broom which he kept in the glove
compartment.

In the sunlight as we search
the beach, your son opens his hand

and asks, "Is this one,
is this greenstone?" Chris,
as you answer, I see in you
without change of atmosphere
my mother. She led the way
into the surf while my father
knocked sand from his shoes.
Your eyes, like hers, are
the same stone, the same blue.

III.

This morning on a hill overlooking the lake, I read Marcel Proust. To
the right, a cliff has collapsed, sending a house to break at the bottom,
window frames smashed on rock, wallpaper naked of roof. This is the
ruin Proust sought, foundation eroded, millionaire's castle broken
into fragments over which he walked with his grandmother who
received whatever misery there was in him with a pity still more vast.
So he could write, "My thoughts were continued in her without having
to undergo any deflection, since they passed from my mind into hers
without change of atmosphere."

Chris, in morning sun from the hill
I watch you escort Proust
up the beach to the train.
Clouds of hawthorne salt the air.
Your way is strewn
with another day's alewives.
I eat eggs sprinkled with sand.

Patricia Hutchings

TO LITTLE GIRLS WHO WOULD BE HORSES

Snorting, pawing at the ground,
I spent my childhood wishing
I was wild and white. I was
a stallion bounding over lawn chairs
in the back yard, my mane
swimming out behind me like a banner.
I mastered all the finest moves
a horse could need to know and
cantered careful figure-eights
into the family lawn.

Charging hilltops, no animal
ever loved its legs like
I did, going through my fancy
gaits on sidewalks of some city park
where no one knew my name
was Thunder.

Lately, I hear the vast Montana herds
are dwindling, pasture lands
fenced in with farms. The mustang
is a dying breed. And as for me,
I find content with smaller scenes:
a circle of brown mares
switching their tails in the fall
sunshine or, today, my golden
daughter making noises to herself,
stamping her hot three-year-old foot
on the back porch, perfect palomino.

HOW TO PAINT WATER

In a pond like a hand
like a hole of mirrors
every tree repeats itself.
Lovers dip their fingers.
Little boys throw stones
through to the other side—
as if it were that simple.
As if we could
just cut, break through
the pretty glittering skin
where the trees live
and the painted clouds.
Inness for instance was
a master of atmosphere but
he never got to the bottom
of water. This seascape
by a child comes closer,
water tipped forward
like Cezanne would want it,
the lake seen through
a cross-section: boats
balanced on the thick top
scalloped line for waves,
great packs of nonspecific
fish, ferns, men
with masks, a black saddled
seahorse. On the bottom
crawling almost off the page
my daughter draws a woman,
her fingers spread wide
as spoons, smiling, teeth
just like a shark.

SO VISION COMES LIKE A RIPE PEACH

We started out believing in a high place,
a hill the fathers took their children up
into the tall grasses where nothing tampered
with the wind and we would lie back
looking up into the hot blue heavens expecting
something we didn't have a name or shape
for then. It was a long summer, that one,

long like waiting for some fancy French dessert,
patiently adding and arranging all the good ingredients,
stirring, getting up one's expectations though
again we had no clear idea, no decent color photograph
of how it ought to look or taste or when
to stop the stirring so it ends up like some thick
exhausted soup until one day, much later, when suddenly

unthinkingly, the fruit is lifted from the bowl
and bitten. It is like nothing we expected,
a peach so sweet one would search forever
and yet suddenly it's here, now, the juice just
rolling down the chin. Amazed, we turn then
to each other, feeling foolish and good
as children, saying: so this is what it was
we were so hungry for.

ANAGNORISIS

Even now we know the ending, waiting
as we are between the acts
for men to rearrange the stage,
move plants and props,
bring in the antique wooden bed
in which an aging man will lie back
in the final scene and speak
few lines. We know that this is
only fiction, some dark vision
of a Russian mind a century before.
You learn to recognize the type.
And so we wait for what's to come
patient, maybe thinking of all the snow
that may have settled since we came,
the chill which falls this time
of night in midwest winter cities
and the cars sending their thin shafts
of light across the ice. They say
this cold is something you get
used to, learning to outlast
the wind and walk on slippery surfaces.
Chekhov would have wanted horses
blowing plumes across the parking lot,
a well-dressed woman settling back
into the carriage seat and suddenly seeing
how the snow makes diamonds
on the driver's dark cloth coat.

WHAT WE SEE BEFORE BREAKFAST

Today we got up early, hoping
some exotic bird had landed
by the river in the night.
Once last year there were
two shining scarlet tanagers,
nearly phosphorescent
in the thick morning light,
the female with a touch
more gentle green but shining
nonetheless. This year
they were nowhere to be seen.
Instead it was a plain brown
thrasher, throwing up the leaves
and bits of dry brush
from last fall, making noise
enough so one could hardly
miss him. Like us, he was
searching for something,
probably with more success.

The rest of the day was drowsy,
lying on the deck discussing
merits of a clear shape
as opposed to sudden bursts
of color in the work of two
well-known recent poets.
We also touched on
the possibility of true
inductive thinking, how one
ever could just see the world
for what it was, without
some kind of predilection
or desire which then
determines what you see
or don't—like the way
looking for a tanager might
sometimes nearly blind one
to the less shocking brown

thrasher, whose shapely
long cinnamon tail is
well worth early rising.

ONE LESS CUSTOMER

The tree may never fall at all
or it may come gently down
at midnight on an empty lawn.
Nevertheless, a good-sized piece
of earth went up and Hiroshima
never even heard it coming.

The world looks rather different
now, the old maps hardly worth
having. Here on Locust Street
where Velda plucks and pops
the hungry black beetles
from her prize petunias
and Ben across the alley
spends the evenings soldering
his junkyard heaven back together
again, a blue sedan might easily
veer and jump the curb when
someone's mother is innocently
walking past, shifting a load
of groceries to the other arm.

AUDEN AND THE ANIMALS

At seventeen he walked out
into the emerald English countryside and cast
his little pile of poems into a large pond.
"Science," he said, "will save the world."
Then there was a myriad of starfish
which he conscientiously cut up and compared
with other early animal forms. At that point,
as in later life, systems were something
he believed in deeply, those intricate
interconnections between one thing
and another he devoted most of his life to
making. Some of these have been preserved,
like the map he made in middle age
in which the history of the western world
is settled in a detailed scheme of struggle
between hell and heaven. He himself
had enormous flaps for ears and nails
bitten back halfway to the moon.
His feet were flat and chronically covered
with large yellow corns which sent him
limping and whining about in gay colors
of carpet slippers he wore almost everywhere.
His students were astounded by his unkempt
dress and also by assignments
where he asked for essays on the day's
events but in reverse or called for them
to memorize the whole of Lycidas.
He counseled all his classes
not to spend their precious years
on being "sensible and cooperative,"
a sin certainly no one could accuse him of.
He changed his mind about almost everything
and often overnight, trying out opinions
like a foreign dish, to see just how
they felt upon the tongue.
Eventually he came to see the ways of God,
the beauty of an early Sunday service
where one has wine without a sermon,

the latter being thoroughly beside the point
since faith was all that really mattered.
Maybe that's the reason he remained so
largely unregenerate in matters of his private life
and even after faith seemed firm was always aching
for an answer that would last longer than the lovers
who came and went so quickly through the years.
The one truth, is there was one,
he believed throughout his life was spoken
best through Caliban, the slave who shows us
how man suffers when the lofty thing
he longs to be must struggle with the animal
he is indeed. For Auden this meant many things
and in the end it meant his death, alone
and drinking in a strange hotel.

Ann Taylor Sargent

from MOTHER AND CHILD TRIPTYCH

I.

I thought the movie camera
came with the first baby.
No, mother said.
She gave it to dad
so he could film Europe.
Before I was even thought of.
Before mother was mother
she sat in a canoe,
slim, animated, watching dad
run film behind an open lens.
She looked straight at him,
straight into the blank eye of the future,
straight into the eyes of her unborn child.
Time drips from her paddle
into a river that runs thirty years,
from that bright day to this dim room.
I watch as she tips her head,
purses her lips around a word.
I can almost hear it.
"Don't," she says.
It sounds different, flirting,
from a woman I never knew,
mother before she was mother.

III.

I built a life to the east of hers,
and as she steps into it, I look again.
The stairs are too steep.
A shock of white hair,
she climbs halfway before resting,
saying, "Don't wait."
She takes half-steps like Matthew,
the boy downstairs.
She lets Matthew in,
gives him bits of pie dough to play with,
plays grandmother to him
as she plays mother to me.
She loves having someone to cook for again.
She loves playing house in my house,
making it smell of pot roast and pie,
of the home that is no longer home
for either of us.
She is small and white
in a tall, dark city.
She is innocent and wistful,
a grandmother waiting for a grandchild,
a motherless child
waiting for her child to be a mother.
Time catches her in its three-way mirror
throwing side-longing glances at the past.

from THE LIGHT FANTASTIC

I.

People are shuffled together
all down the granite avenue.
Everything is gray and dirty.
Then my eyes take in the flags,
flying like fresh laundry overhead.
They are drenched with sunlight,
dripping with color.
Saturated, fluid.
They lean out from second stories
like nosy housewives.

III.

Shade, like an evening tide,
almost fills the space
between the rows of brownstones.
A slow glint of sunlight
touches the neighbor's top floor window
and turns to swim one last lap
down into the darkness.
The light is soft and wrinkled,
as from water.
It swims through an east window,
fingers an inner wall.
Like a deep-sea diver,
searching a sunken ship.
Like a piece of tarnished treasure,
it sinks back into the shadows.

LOCKED IN

In Brooklyn,
in the middle of a quiet block,
in the middle of a quiet day,
Carmen, surrounded on all sides,
raises her voice three stories.
Her son has tripped the back door lock,
trapping them in their own little yard.
Their rowhouse takes sides
with other houses circling round them.
Their fence links arms
with a chain of neighbors' fences.
Their yard is one tooth
in a perfect set of clenched teeth.
Carmen, locked in her own back yard,
raises her voice three stories,
hoping to open a window.

TO THE MUSIC MAKER

Bales of hay
stand out across the field
like nubs
on a music box roll.

It takes a day
to reap a song.
It takes the sun
all day to play across it.

GETHSEMANE

Lilies of the valley
of the garden of death know:
wimpled heads bow
in garden's convent.
They are sisters of garlic,
in essence God-fathered.
Flower cups, spilt of their blood,
shroud paled hearts.

I'll martyr a few
for our supper tonight,
wash my hands and
the garlic's feet—take, eat!
They our table grace,
with scent atone for spice.

LINES ON LINEN AND CANVAS

Degas painted her, and Picasso—
the nameless woman, ironing.
Pressing out wrinkles
with a hot, heavy hand.
Half-hearing the steam's hiss,
the iron's thump.
Half-smelling the oil
that hangs in the damp air.
Half-forgetting the man in the corner
who puts lines on cloth as deliberately
as she irons them out.

Soft strokes in the corner,
sable brushes in uncalloused hands.
They lay a real woman on the clean canvas.
We can see where her arm moved.
We can see the hunched stance,
the abstract gaze, the drab coloring.
He paid his model nothing, poor man,
not in money, not in flattery.
Posterity has paid him well.
His image of her endures.

And her image of him?
As they watched each other work,
what did her indifferent eyes see?
A fool? A man intense in his work?
Or just a need for clean, pressed smocks?

No one needs a pressed shirt,
no one needs a painting.
We can walk around wrinkled,
blinking at blank walls.
But we will pay a little
for linens smooth and white.
We will pay to see a canvas
smooth and stretched and stained.

Their images hang
on a whitewashed wall.
We file past
in our best permapress
and throw glances like flowers
on their grave.
The one who mistrusted art
is enshrined with it.
She would approve
of the care and the cleanliness.

ANNUAL OUTING

Each spring,
lilacs and apple trees
invite us to visit.
Like great aunts, over-rouged,
like maiden aunts in floral chintz
they kiss us
with sweet cheap perfume.
Perched on doilies of shade,
they preside over picnics.
We lounge on lawn
as plush and prickly
as old upholstery.
We pay our respects,
pleased to see them
so civilized, so similar
to the way they were
last spring.

MINUET IN MANNERS

She was leaving
the office building
as he entered.
Her right hand pressed open
the lobby door
just as his pushed in
the outside one.
Then came the hesitation step—
each held the door
for the other.
After pausing,
they swung past,
back to back,
exchanging places,
reaching for the other door
with the other hand.
Perfect timing,
like trapeze artists.
It was like watching
a do-si-do with double doors.
Found choreography.

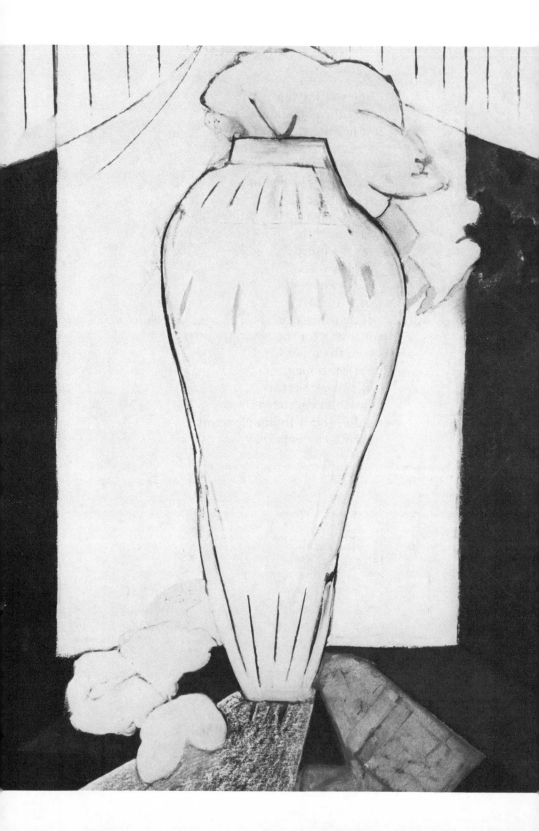

William Meissner

ALL THE HORSES

I watch her as she stares into the cupboard. Stares. Into the cupboard. There's plenty of food where she's looking: jars of spaghetti, canned peas, mushroom soup, peaches, and still room left over for echoes. She's standing there, staring into the cupboard, and in that long silence I hear hooves.

The dream. I begin to remember the wild horses. The dream begins to seep back into my skin again. How could I have forgotten it? Galloping. What do they want?

I want to tell her the can of red tomato sauce we'd been storing in the refrigerator has turned black around the edges. That's not what I hoped for—a black halo around the rim like a festering sore.

I remember the horses biting at each other with long yellow teeth as they gallop in the mud of a shallow riverbed. I know the two lead horses love each other, but they still bite deep into each other's skin. Red circles open on their flanks. Their necks stretch again and again, biting. Their teeth protrude like old piano keys, and there is the music of hooves in tepid water.

The spaghetti noodles boil and boil. The ground beef smells bad. Did we leave it out too long? This tomato sauce—should we use it? I'd like to ask her, but she's not looking at me. Her eyes are opening a cupboard door, closing a cupboard door. I would like to ask her. It takes the strength of all my muscles, my mud-splattered muscles, to drag the words from my throat.

"The tomato sauce. Should we use it?" She does not answer for ten seconds, or a year.

The horses' muzzles are flecked with mud as they race in slow motion, fog curling around them like memories too thick to see through. What are they trying to leave behind?

Once she told me how her fourth grade students frustrated her at school until she wanted to throw herself through the second—story window:

"Take the circle apart to see how many pieces you have, Sheri. That's it. Now how many are there?"

"Two."

"Good. So then what fraction does one piece equal?"

"I dunno," the girl shrugged, her eyes china plates.

"You know it's a fraction. What do you think it equals?"

"One-third?"

"No, Sheri." The window. "Try again, Sheri. Now *think* this time."

"Two-thirds?"

The window. Three hundred sixty degrees. "Put the pieces back together into a circle, then let's try taking it apart again . . ."

"Yes, let's use it."

"But it's blackening around the edges," I mutter.

"Huh?"

The dream again: now there's fire rising up from the water, dark smoke filling the air. One horse comes leaping through the bright flame. Another horse. Another. For a moment one horse's flowing white mane catches fire. Water and fire. The horse shakes its head into the wind and keeps running.

Once she said to me, "The only relationship that doesn't hurt is a superficial one. The minute you let a person get one grain under your skin, it begins to fester."

A horse stumbles, breaking its own leg. He falls to the riverbed, is trampled by the galloping herd behind him. Thousands of horses, millions of hooves. Soon he is nothing more than a dark, quivering mound. What are they running toward? What are they running from? How much can they lose?

"Put it in anyway," she finally blurts.

So I pour the sauce into the frying pan, and stir, trying to erase the blackness.

The blackness of the smoke as the horses charge head-first into it, through it. This dream I've been having for five years and never knowing it, never remembering an instant of it.

"Did you set the timer?"

I keep thinking she's not serious, keep thinking she can't mean all this. Can't believe she's deciding to take our circle apart and throw the pieces away.

Spheres of mud the size of eyeballs fly into the air, land on a beach as the horses rear and shift direction mid-gallop when they near the fire. One huge gray horse seems to be trying to inhale all the smoke into his nostrils. I imagine it forming little tornados inside his body as he breathes in the swirling, swirling blackness.

"I think we've overcooked the noodles," I try to say. In my mind I smash a plate against the sink. Spheres of mud fly into the air. I feel grains of sand crawl under the skin of my arm.

Now, somehow, I can see the end of the dream: one by one the horses leap into the water, the water. They break through the cold window of water to quench the burning inside their bellies, to stop the smoke, the fire. All these years. Why didn't I know? The dream of wild horses—it's all being extinguished now by the whiteness of deep water. Lips of water open slowly around their plunging bodies, cool white crowns of foam rise.

The buzzer on the stove boils in my ears as the horses sink out of sight. Their manes, flowing like noodles, are last to go under. The echoes of hooves.

"It's done," I say. She does not answer. "Something's done."

I watch her standing in front of the cupboard again, staring long minutes, as if she doesn't exactly know what it was she wanted there.

MOTHER, FATHER AND SON

1. Mother. From Milk to Poison

Her exact height is not important. What is important is that she stands about as high as the fifth shelf of the storage closet in her kitchen. The shelf is piled with empty containers: mayonnaise jars, jelly jars, Mason jars, liquor bottles, plastic whipping cream cups. Even some old dark plastic containers that could have hidden everything from milk to poison; over the years she's forgotten which are which.

When the contents of a container in the house are emptied, the Mother washes it with soap and hot water, grinding off all the tiny impurities that might be clinging to the sides or bottom. She stares straight ahead and scrubs the jar a few minutes until it is spotless. Then she rinses it with clear, steaming water. She holds it to the kitchen light. "There, not a speck."

Then she places a jar on a shelf in the kitchen closet. "Use all three words when you talk about that room," she used to say when her son referred to it. She positions the jar delicately, the fingers of both hands clasped around it. She lifts the jar above the shelf, then lowers it, slowly, down to the wooden boards. As if she were lowering a small coffin carefully so that she would not disturb the body inside.

Below the fifth shelf are four other shelves covered from back to front with containers. And the spare room upstairs. And the basement. The jars and cups and boxes all gawk at the ceiling with open mouths. Webs stretch across some of them, tiny silken tightropes.

"Don't leave them on the stairs," the Mother says to her son. "Take them all the way down. How would your dad or I ever see our way down?"

Somehow, these rooms are still hollow, thinks the Mother. And she is on her way up or down the stairs with her arms crossed in front of her abdomen clutching another load of containers.

No, the Mother does not know her actual height. She has not thought of that in years; somewhere along the way it has been rinsed from her mind. When she smiles she parts her lips to leave an empty space. She knows she is about as tall as the dark fifth shelf in her kitchen storage closet, and she lowers another jar balanced between her white fingertips.

2. The Father. Will He Stop?

The Father is concerned about his weight. He is nearly six feet tall, but his broadness through the middle and hip makes him seem much shorter. The Mother is bothered by the fact that he refuses to step on the bathroom scale.

He is part German, and he has a mouth that changes shape often; it has a mind of its own. His eyes are narrow graves and his broad brow occasionally wrinkles tight like a fist. He is balding, and he no longer speaks of his hair, or why it decided to jump from his head.

The Father's favorite possession is Eva. He will tell you that Eva is a remarkable white-furred little dog—she sits up, rolls over, leaps through the hoop of his arms, and barks on a signal. But she also does one other trick; this trick is the Father's pride—he calls it Eva's greatest trick—and he will make her do it for any visitors and, most of all, for the family members themselves.

On a Sunday afternoon, Eva sat quietly on the linoleum while the family was finishing a roast chicken dinner. The Father then stared at Eva; his deep-set eyes always found her after a good meal. The Father picked up a white scrap of chicken that he had saved on the side of his dinner plate. He stepped next to Eva, and held the chicken high over her head. She knew; her nose twitched; her eyes tensed hard like beads.

Then it came: he gave the command for her greatest trick. It was loud; it jabbed the air of the kitchen, echoed in the jars in the storage closet.

"Dad, no," said the Mother.

The command was repeated.

"Dad, Oh Dad."

The dog did not move.

The Father repeated the command: "Eva! Sneeze!"

The dog stepped rapidly from one small foot to the other as if she were dancing on a hot griddle. He repeated the command. Again. Each time, the Father's voice became shriller. Each time his pupils bounced, black bullets. Suddenly, out of her circles of frustration, Eva let loose a sharp bark.

"Give it to her now," whined the Mother.

He turned toward the Mother for a moment; his stare found her pleading smile and tore at it, tore at it, until it shredded and disappeared. He turned back to the dog. And then, quickly, "Eva! Sneeze!"

"Oh Dad, stop. Why doesn't he stop that?" she asked the Son, who had heard the commands from the living room and walked in. "Oh I wish he would stop," she repeated to no one.

In another moment, it was all over. The Father gnawed on his upper lip; the scowl was as if two snakes were wrestling. He grunted with finality at the dog: "Then you don't get this!" He held the piece of meat high above his forehead and turned his back.

"Oh Dad!" the Mother groaned behind him. But he heard nothing; he had left the room, stepped into the bathroom, and closed the door partially behind him. The piece of chicken landed with a plunk in the toilet bowl; it sank through the water, a pale wing. Then he flushed the toilet and walked out.

3. The Son. Yes, every day.

His height and weight are not important. Let us call him a young man of average height, with a slightly slim build. He would say that he knows his height and weight perfectly: "They are 6 feet ¼ inch and 155 respectively." But do not believe him, he does not really know for sure.

He will also tell you that everything has been fine for him since that day. True, he does have his annual hay fever when he sneezes frequently from August 15th (it always begins on that exact day his Mother said it would begin) to October 25th, but he will tell you it is nothing, really nothing.

What is important is that he is away from home now, and has been away for two years since that day. He is off and running on his own, he will tell you, and he has made new friends, has found a great job, and lots of girls. He will admit that he occasionally gets letters from his mother. She will fill up one page with thick handwriting that complains about the Father and then, at the bottom: "Love, Mother and Father."

And he might even admit that he occasionally receives stamped, sealed envelopes addressed to him that are completely empty. They're postmarked in his home town, miles away. He's not positive, but he thinks that his Mother might be sending them. He slides these envelopes into his desk; he keeps them orderly with a white rubber band. He will tell you that he keeps them there just as a record of how many he's received. After two years, the desk drawers are full of them. He may tell you that actually he has no idea who could be sending them.

Besides his new job and friends, he also has a pet bird. The bird is a mutation—a white parakeet that the Son calls Shadow. He likes the name—shadows make a person feel more comfortable, he will tell you. Shadows contain you better than light does.

Every afternoon the Son sits in a shadow in the corner of his room. He makes the bird Shadow sit there with him also, on his lap. The bird shivers and does not move.

While he sits in the shadow each day, the Son thinks of his room at home, and how he kept two jars on top of the wooden dresser. They were filled to the brim with dimes and pennies, he remembers—he had collected them for years and years. But that day he emptied them, dumped the pennies and dimes into a cloth bag so he could spend them once he left home. Forty-two dollars and fifty-two cents. He wishes he had those two jars now, here in his apartment. But this time he would keep them empty, he thought, so he could see his eyes reflect in them.

Some days he remembers what happened during the last five minutes on that day he finally left home. His mother had noticed the empty jars on the dresser, and her long fingers circled them. "Here," she told him, "take these to the basement." He heard his father, outside the room, asking about the packed suitcase in the hallway. Suddenly the Son grabbed the jars from her and smashed them against the wall.

It was like a bubble that had been rising to the surface for years, and he opened his mouth wide to blurt it to them: "I'm going!"

"Leaving?" she asked weakly.

"You're going nowhere," his father shouted. The Son dragged the suitcase past them. "Do you hear me? You sit down in that living room!"

"Careful on those stairs!" he heard the Mother call. "How will you ever see your own way down?"

Every day for an hour, the Son pulls the shadows over him like a black plastic sheet and thinks about that last Sunday. Before he knows it, his time is up; he remembers that the mail will arrive soon, wonders if he will receive another envelope. He keeps a rubber band tight around his wrist.

He wonders if the Mother will receive the first white envelope from him in her mail today. He pictures her, tearing it open, the Father looking impatiently over her shoulder as her fingers climb up and down the jagged paper stairway of its emptiness.

Jeffrey Stockwell

MEMORY OF A WING

I was on the University of Minnesota Gymnastic team from 1972 to 1976. My friend Blair Hanson worked the high bar—it was his specialty. He graduated the year I came in, but he returned often to work-out and help us novices. It was in preparation for an alumni meet that he suffered a fall that left him paralyzed, and a month later he died. "The Memory of a Wing" is a series of six poems, dedicated to Blair, centered on the six Olympic events of men's gymnastics.

Floor Exercise

(In Floor Exercise look for tumbling movements: front, back, and twisting flips. A gymnast will also include a move requiring strength and others demonstrating flexibility and balance.)

in preparation we stretch each part of the body
enjoying the leisure of cows
legs beside us like eagle wings
air wells up from the valley
and we begin
tumbling like stones over the surface of the water
in the corners we rest
then perform the leaps of dolphins
weaving the waves together
that message of joy
to sailors who slid lifeless into the sea

we are horses
striding around each other
our strong shoulders
lift us from the ground
weightless
we receive the gift of feathers

on the tip of a woman's breast
taste the sea
hearing scatter
like burning chips from a welder's iron

he lifts her body
silence pours down from her hair
hips touch
like hands cupped together to hold water

Vaulting

(The vaulter wants to fly as high and as far as he can—with good form).

I start from the same place
steps wait for me like tracks in the sand
each breath comes from a distance
and has the face of someone I know

I climb on top of my back
stare at the board
the gate opens
I run
five steps from the board
my eyes close
I lift into the memory of a wing
this is the place
where I will bring my pain
if I stay
I will see the sun
that rose before I was born

I land in the soft blue mats

I have faith
that I will always
catch myself singing

Pommel Horse

(The pommel horse is a difficult event because even the smallest mistake breaks the routine's flow. The gymnast must perform circling movements with legs together, as well as scissor moves with legs apart.)

before I start
fragments of past routines come together in my mind
each trick alive
as a hawk with its wings open

arms locked and strong
like the white falls
that hold the mountain over its own reflection
I squeeze the pommels
and ride that animal beneath me
my body
stiff as a penguin
swings round and round up the mountain
the weight of my legs disappear
I am just ahead of my self
it is amazing the way clouds move
it is amazing the way my feet
enjoy the water like fish

a herd of white goats
moves up the mountain

spring
each hoof finds its balance on the high cliffs

summer
grass against the roof of the mouth

fall
fur twists with the wind

winter
the sun sinks into the snow
sky flames red
the spirits of animals
move across the shoulders of the mountains

Still Rings

(A ring routine includes both strength and swinging moves while the rings remain as still as possible.)

two cables hang from the ceiling
strapped to the end of each is a wooden ring
who will take the bait
and risk the excitement of a child
who touches the leaves at the peak of his swing
this is a safe place
where the hands become feet

on a calm night
walk to the edge of the land
sail
with the wind that fills our bodies

Blair I watched you at your death
your tongue became a white star
you are my navigator
I can see
the leaping porpoises
tattooed to your back

you said
"at dusk
follow the birds
they will return to their island nest
in the night
use the star path
follow the one on the horizon
when it has moved too high
follow the next to rise from the same point"

we reach the island
our bodies become statues
unable to tell the living the path we have traveled

crabs on the beach burrow into the sand
terns feed along the white lace of the waves

Parallel Bars

(Like the rings, the parallel bars require great upper body strength.
Moves should be performed both above and below the bars.)

the sun reveals the galaxy of dust
that drifts in the gym

some days there is an empty nest
in everyone's mood
their eyes stare out from
the darkside of the ground
you must work your way out
grip the bars and pull youself into the balance of a handstand
swing into the currents of dust

each routine is a journey
to a special place
the rails become condor wings
that open over the ocean

there are still moments
when you can see the desert
three cows buried in the sand
their bones
the faint outline of constellations
sometimes at dusk
we are just silhouettes
our bodies outline with light
as if the sun was at our feet
a child
we bend down to
and so
we rotate in a current of gravity
it is hard to die
because we are birds
who know the joy of falling

Horizontal Bar

(Watch for the gymnast to circle the bar in both directions and to release and recatch the bar several times before throwing a spectacular dismount.)

the hands are rubbed with white chalk
ceremony for protection
the bar is eight feet above the floor

the way a pianist draws music into her hands
the movement of your body
can take you for miles
each step you get closer to your shadow
a bird that follows the river

Blair
gravity took your neck under its powerful arm

you did not spin fast enough
your skin gave up its color
your father leaned over you
his arms oars
the bed floats out on the river
rowing away from this life
the snow on the mountain
is the only cloud in the sky

your dream as a child
jumping from your mother's bed
you could fly with the balance of wings
over your brother and sister
you told them you could live alone
then night came
the black face of a hyena
the moon a flamingo in its mouth

I confess father
I have spoken to others
with your voice
now
I call to the living every time you speak

sea turtles travel each year
to the edge of the water
two lovers land from the waves
they slip out of their protection
and lay in the sand
in the blossom of their struggle
eggs appear
the young break through
their leather wings hook the lip of a wave
then disappear beneath the white surf

Joel Helgerson

from THE SPARROW NEST GANG

"A Late Night Tavern Conversation"

Barns the empty-glassed sports reporter said to Lefty, "It's a shame and an outrage and blasphemous, and it hurts me deep down in here Lefty, deep down." He patted his chest over his heart. "And don't think it doesn't hurt deep down."

Lefty said to Barns, "All right, I didn't mean it."

Barns the unforgiving sports reporter said to Lefty, "No, O no, no, no, you meant it all right. We've known each other a long time Lefty, and this I never expected."

Lefty said to Barns, "I take it all back, every word."

Barns the relentless sports reporter said to Lefty, "You'd like to, wouldn't you? Yes, O yes, yes, yes. But that's just the point: Lies linger on as long as the truth."

Lefty said to Barns, "I was joking. Forget I said it, that's all."

Barns the defenseless sports reporter said to Lefty, "Deep down," and patted his chest.

Lefty said to Barns, "I didn't mean any of it."

"Really?"

"Really."

Barns the true-friend sports reporter said to Lefty, "I didn't think you did."

Tulips

One month out of every year Penny danced exotically at the Golden Goose. The month of May, when tulips bloomed, Penny danced. Her costume consisted of tulip pasties and a three tulip G-string.

The month of May was when Lefty first learned of the Golden Goose through Alvin the parking-lot attendant. Penny was Alvin's roommate.

Penny always came and talked to Lefty between her acts, and so Lefty soon met the other strippers, and so he rather liked the Golden Goose. He felt like a father to Penny, and he worried about what would become of her because Alvin was not always a nice person.

One night Penny told Lefty why she stayed with Alvin. Her story helped Lefty to explain to himself why he stayed with baseball: It was a game he could cry over.

Alvin and Penny were not particularly happy living on Alvin's salary, but this had more to do with Alvin's lack of grace than lack of money. Alvin had a habit of mentioning tulips and the month of May in the same tone of voice with which he mentioned Cadillac owners who didn't tip.

"Leave the creep," Gina Bonbon told her. "Work up an act for the other eleven months of the year and leave the creep."

Penny wouldn't even consider leaving Alvin because he was the only man she'd ever known who could cry.

"There aren't many such men" she told Gina, "and when a woman finds one she shouldn't mind the bad stuff because the good stuff is so good. Have you ever had a man lay his head down on your lap and bawl like a baby? If you had, you'd know."

Penny had thought of expanding her act so that she and Alvin would have more money, but it had taken her a long time to conceive of her tulip motif, and no other suggested theme equaled the tulips.

For her breasts, she preferred red tulips with sunshine stains on the petals' insides. The G-string tulips had to be yellow, pure yellow, with no stains. One of the the G-string tulips had to have an entire stem so that she could ease the stem inside herself. With the stem inside her, she had enough security to perform in front of crowds. At the end of her act she gently tugged out the entire tulip, presenting it to the shyest gentleman in the crowd.

One night Alvin stormed into the Golden Goose, liquored up and loaded with troubles. Penny was halfway through her act. Two roly-poly brothers from South Dakota sat in the front row with the pasty tulips covering their noses. Alvin tried to remove these tulips with his knuckles; the brothers tried removing Alvin with their knuckles. Penny cried all the way to her dressing room.

"Leave him," Gina said.

"I can't. He's my only man."

That night she didn't let Alvin touch her, nor did she let him touch her for the next week. She didn't go work even though the manager of the Golden Goose called twice and tried to coax her back. In the mornings she felt sick as she listened to Alvin make his lunch box. At night, while worrying about where Alvin went after work, she tried to ignore the cravings she had for strawberry shortcake on top of watermelon.

When Alvin got home, he said:

"I don't like you up on that bar. I don't want you to do it no more. You stay here with me where you're wanted." His voice weaseled through the bandages covering his nose and made Penny afraid of what he might do next.

Not until May ended and Alvin put his head on Penny's lap to ask for forgiveness—tears settling down his cheeks—not until then did Penny relent. When she heard him crying up there on the surface of her body, she crawled out from deep inside herself, where she had been listening to Gina's advice echo over and over. Seeing Alvin cry again made her realize what a lucky woman she was.

They helped each other into the bedroom as if invalids. Helpless at removing their own clothes, they fussed with the other's clothes. At last they lay on the bed as they had done before. Alvin's head rested on her abdomen. Although he had stopped crying, Penny imagined that he continued.

"Penny, you forgot to take your tulip out."

Which started them giggling and laughing, with each getting excited about the naked body next to them, as they giggled and laughed.

"How long's that been in there?"

"Since you busted up my act, I guess."

"That's over a week."

"I forgot."

Alvin tried tugging on it, but it stayed firm.

"God, that's tight."

He yanked on it and Penny cried:

"Careful! Careful!"

Fifteen minutes later he still hadn't gotten that tulip to budge. He'd lubricated it, cajoled it, and pleaded with it in ancient, unknown languages. In the end he collapsed from the effort, laying his head on Penny's stomach, which remained tense from the attempted uprooting.

"Alvin, I promise I'll never dance at the Golden Goose again."

Then Alvin cried, and Penny ran her fingers through his tousled hair.

"It is a beautiful yellow tulip, isn't it," Penny agreed, happy to have a man who could appreciate such things.

The Gift of an Arm

Early in the season the Sparrow Nest Gang held every first but first place. Some people accused them of having the game's first cybernetic throwing arm. Pressures had mounted after the first four weeks of the season because Colonel Nakayama bought a badly needed third baseman.

Rifle Walker had played in the league for twenty years, had announced his retirement the year before because of a sore arm, but Colonel Nakayama's offer lured him back.

Twenty years of living on the road had made Rifle a private man. He roomed alone. He didn't shower with the team. If anyone wanted to shake his hand, he only nodded. On the question of how his arm became young again, he said nothing.

The one person he talked to was Billy the bat boy. Billy didn't prod him with questions about his arm.

Everyone talked to Billy. Billy had pitched brilliantly for the Yankees until beaned by a fast ball that permanently gave him the mind of a child. Everyone had a little of the Billy-fear when they stepped into the batter's box. Add to this the crippling of an arm in a recent auto crash, and everyone talked to Billy because they were ashamed not to—Rifle Walker included.

Another week dragged by. Reporters interviewed Rifle's wife: No, she had nothing to say.

A reporter visited Rifle's mother in Boone, Iowa: She couldn't believe it.

Rifle's neighbors were interviewed: They trusted that Rifle would do the right thing.

Rifle's new coach cautiously put it this way during a meal one night:

"Is that thing sticking our your sleeve a real arm, or is it a tinker-toy?"

Yet for the first time all season they won games regularly. With Rifle sewing shut the hole at third, the team began to function. Yumio Utsugi and Susie Dugan worked the shortshop to second base double-play to computer perfection. Stretch Washington, the first baseman, made the long reaches for those hurrying double-play tosses. And when Rifle zipped the ball to Stretch from third, the ball had so much mustard on it that Stretch took to removing his glove after a putout and blowing on his hand.

On the day that the Detroit team hired a helicopter to hover over third base with a suspended magnet, all hell broke loose.

In the third inning the Sparrow Nest Gang refused to go out onto the field. The roar of the copter's blades made it impossible for the players to talk to each other. Nor could Billy get the sparrows excited because they couldn't hear him pounding.

"I've had it!" Payday Woods shouted in the locker room after the forfeit. "I won't play under these conditions."

The rest of the team tensed. With the helicopter gone, they heard Billy walloping the bleacher seats, they heard the sparrows. Billy created a stir over by the first baseline, coming closer. With no fans to absorb the energy that Billy created, the commotion of the sparrows keyed them up.

"I want to know what that arm of yours is!" Payday shouted.

At which point Billy barged into the locker room, sopping wet from his exertion, rapping his bat on benches and lockers. The collision of Payday's shout and Billy's frenzy ignited a brawl that included the entire team, except for Yumio Utsugi who sat untouched in a corner.

A photographer snapped a picture which assured the Sparrow Nest Gang of keeping its feisty image. Payday Woods wrestled with Rifle Walker, neither gaining an advantage. Stretch Washington had headlocks on two relief pitchers that had tried ripping off Rifle's sweat shirt.

It took a sudden, piercing shout from Yumio Utsugi to stop everything: "Ya-oooo!!!"

He stood on top of a bench, concentrating on a dandelion, which he pinched with his fingers. The spinning of the dandelion—contrasted with his screech—dumbfounded everyone. The room became still, with everyone looking at Yumio. He said:

"You all wonder where Rifle got his right arm. Have none of you wondered how Billy lost his right arm?"

Someone muttered, "Jesus Christ."

Payday Woods pushed Rifle away, and everyone went to sit in front of their lockers as if some answer hung on a hook next to their clothes.

Billy became excited. He touched two players on the shoulder, but they wouldn't turn around.

"This team could win a World Championship," Billy said. "I know it could. That's all I wanted. My arm's a good arm, it could help."

None of the players could forget Billy's plea, and at their next stop, Denver, they swept a three game series.

Two No-Names

The left and center fielders of the Sparrow Nest Gang had a tranquil May and June compared to the ballyhoo that went on in right field between Payday Woods and the fans. Payday delighted in giving odds on the Sparrow's chances for the pennant. "Plenty good if we got some pitching." The fans threw ticket stubs at Payday while complaining of the price of their seats. And during all this the left and center fielders protected the tranquillity of their separate pastures by playing steady ball. Lefty took to calling them the sheepherders.

"Those two sheepherders," Lefty told Barns the sports reporter, "are the only steady influences on this team."

Not long after Lefty mentioned this to Barns some ugly rumors concerning the sheepherders began circulating throughout the league. The kind of rumors that sheepherders have had to tolerate since ancient Greece. The fact that they bunked together on road trips may have fostered these libels, or the mistake that Lefty made in using the analogy of sheepherders to Barns may have triggered the rumors, but, regardless of origins, the Sparrows now had to live with whisperers who whispered that Jack Williamson and Pepe Gold-tooth Morales were in love.

Lefty took the two of them aside in Cleveland and suggested that they make a public statement.

"Both to clear your names and for the sake of the team."

It was at that point that Lefty noticed two things: One, neither William-son nor Morales had answered him; two, Jack had his arm warmly around Pepe's shoulder.

"We coodn't do such a statement," Pepe said.

During the following pause Lefty began to wonder why they couldn't make such a statement. They weren't shy boys; in truth, they had publicly complained about their obscurity on such a media swamped team. Barns the sports reporter had explained the number one rule of journalism to them (. . . all the news that's fit to stink) and had suggested they do something news-worthy. But Jack and Pepe didn't become flamboyant. They weren't disloyal players; actually, they'd played above their talents all season. They had no one to shield but themselves by refusing to make a statement. Then Lefty began to feel helpless because they could only be protecting themselves. Lefty thought that he had slid past the age of feeling anger behind his cheeks, but now he felt firebirds behind his cheeks, while honor and tradition quaked in his stomach. He did contain himself long enough to ask:

"Have you two boys talked to a minister?"

Pepe smiled his fourteen carat smile, but Jack took this question serious-ly and pointed out to Lefty that this wasn't a shoddy one-night stand—it was love—and he also reminded Lefty that he had claimed they were the only steady influence on the team. "You wouldn't want to upset our balance, would you Lefty?"

"Naut our balances," Pepe agreed.

"In fact," Jack continued, "we had been meaning to make an announcement."

All of which made Lefty blusteringly mad. Out of his office he ordered them. Banished, excommunicated, deported . . . these words he sputtered, and not until Pepe smiled on the way out and said, "Doon't worry Left, we'll still catch your fly balls," did Lefty realize that what felt like fire on the inside of his cheeks must have looked like crimson embarrassment on the outside.

Waiting for the newspaper guillotine to fall had Lefty fidgeting for two weeks, but Jack and Pepe never held their press conference; they did each con-tinue to play steady ball, and now they held hands when they came in off the playing field. Photographers made the most of that.

A Cooperstown devotee discovered that the bubble-gum card showing the Sparrows as a team also showed Williamson's arm around Pepe's waist. Fathers ripped up that card and put basketball hoops up over garage doors.

The Commissioner sent a special request to Colonel Nakayama (who forwarded it to Lefty) that said that nothing less than the manliness of an entire institution was at stake. Something had better be done.

A National League star threatened to sue a cosmetic company if they went ahead and aired a television commercial he'd made for a women's perfume.

Certain boys clubs began to appear at Sparrow games where they threw kisses and cheered extravagantly for Pepe and Jack.

The national pride of Venezuela (Pepe's home) was threatened, and Catholic computers in heaven registered enough prayers and lighted candles for Pepe's eternal soul to fill two or three saint's quotas for the year.

Through all of which Lefty silently waited for Pepe and Jack's press conference, which would clear up everyone's doubts and make every traditional fan wish that modern day players had a whole closet full more of discretion.

Lefty put off talking to them again not because he balked at the pressures the Colonel put on him, but because he didn't know if he could control himself. This was one of those duties that he usually put off and put off, secretly hoping the situation would change but actually knowing that it grew worse, but this time it changed:

Lefty had been anonymously depositing sacks of mail outside Pepe and Jack's hotel rooms—mail from little leaguers, mail from church elders, mail from Venezuela. He hoped it would show them how important it was for a baseball player to at least appear to be a man. He'd just dropped off another pay load when Pepe opened the door. Awkwardly, Lefty pretended that he was picking up the mail sack rather than setting it down. Pepe didn't notice.

"Left," Pepe said, "cood you arrange for another roommate for my person? Maybe me and Jack don't love each other any more."

Which gave Lefty one electric jolt, but he didn't have to tell Pepe it was for the best because Pepe closed the door.

After a time of continued reasoning that he wasn't at fault for the break-up and that it was for the best, Lefty grew tired of waiting for a chance to tell Pepe and Jack that such decisions sometimes had to be made. He went to Pepe's room to tell him directly. He had practiced for two days exactly what he wanted to say when the time came, and of course he forgot exactly what he wanted to say when the time did come. (He wanted to explain that the sacrifice that Pepe and Jack had made was appreciated by one Lefty Schmidky, if no one else.)

The hotel door opened and Pepe faced him with his fourteen carat smile because he'd made a spectacular somersault catch that day that had won the game. All those words of explanation that Lefty had practiced zoomed right into the invisible distance.

Lefty breathed deep twicely, then said:

"I don't know if you'll believe this, Pepe, but I'm sorry about you and Jack. The two of you looked happy together. I kind of got used to your holding hands in front of all the fans. It seemed like the thing a man might do."

So Jack and Pepe had quit holding hands and they had new roommates. None of the old Sparrows said a thing about it. It was one topic the team seemed eager to forget, although everyone did hurry in and out of the showers. (That meant no team members missed airplanes, which pleased the Colonel.)

The rumors continued but gradually weakened until chicken broth was stronger than the rumors and tasted better to gossips.

Snailball

The Boston team was notorious for stealing bases. They slid with their spikes up. They took second basemen out of double-plays with hard body blams. They publicly vowed to wipe out the Sparrows with sharp cleats and blinding speed.

No one on the Sparrow Nest Gang took the hype seriously; no one except Lefty. He brooded over the threats.

"They can't steal on us!" He cried to himself at night.

After the first game in Boston, the rest of the Sparrows took the threats seriously too. The Red Sox stole six bases, cleated Rifle Walker, knocked the wind out of Yumio in an attempted double-play, and they won the game 4 to 0.

On the bus back to their hotel the entire team became dispirited. Billy the bat boy said, "Geez you guys, you gotta win this next one." But no one wanted to talk to Billy. He went from one team member to another during the bus ride and not a one of them had a thing to say to him. At last Billy sat down next to Lefty, who normally wouldn't have let Billy take the empty seat after a losing game.

"Lefty, we gotta do something. Can you think of anything to do?"

Lefty had been thinking. He knew that in the next game it was a must to stop the Red Sox from stealing bases. If they stole bases tomorrow, then the whole league would begin stealing against them. From Casey Steelgut came instructions on how to hold base runners closer to the bag, but Lefty sensed that this would not be enough. Boston was fast and Squat Tomko didn't have the best throwing arm in the league. The reason that teams hadn't run on the Sparrows until now was that they'd been able to win in safer ways.

The next morning Lefty took Billy with him as he checked out several pet shops and several gift shops. He bought several types of sea shells, which he had Billy step on when they were outside.

"Like this, Lefty?" Billy brought his heel down hard on a rose colored scallop shell.

"That's fine."

The shell cracked on Billy's second try, and Lefty inspected the remains of the shell; then he shook his head no.

They continued checking in and out of pet shops and gift shops. Lefty bought shells, and Billy asked, "Like this?"; and Lefty kept saying "That's fine." Lefty bought clam shells, sand dollars, small abalone shells, and a fingernail-sized starfish. Billy gave each of them his heel.

In a bead and necklace shop, Lefty bought a necklace made of snail shells. The shells were shiny and dainty, and Billy seemed reluctant to bring his foot down on the tiny snail homes.

"Go ahead, Billy. The snail doesn't need it any more."

Still Billy hesitated so that when he brought his foot down he did it as lightly as possible. The shell popped, which startled Billy into jerking his foot away.

"That was loud."

Lefty knelt down and touched the small, brittle pieces left on the pavement.

"That will do just fine," he said, patting Billy on the back. "I think our problems are solved." He went back into the shop and bought a second necklace so that he would have a reserve supply.

That afternoon at the game he instructed Yumio Utsugi and Stretch Washington to secretly place snail shells on top of first and second base and on the running paths.

When Boston's runners rounded a base, they heard a pop and felt the crackling, which was just enough to make them look back and slow down the step that stopped them from stretching singles into doubles or from stealing bases on Squat's weak arm.

Not that such a ploy could last forever, but it made Lefty feel like a manager. It had him whistling in the dugout.

Ron Ellis

FRED KROMER

Once through the pneumatic doors I go numb
in the empire of the utterly practical, where grim
do-it-yourselfers quest among the name-brands,
plod with bored feet between stacks of lumber.
Taking my number, I watch them dodge fork-lifts
and read prices cynically, resigned to chicanery.
Fred Kromer is the name on his tag. "Fred,
what's the best way to cut galvanized roofing?"
"You got a radial saw? Well, take a dull old
combination blade," he said, "put it on backwards,
you know, wrong side out? It'll cut most any metal."
"You mean I won't have to buy a special blade?"
"Why no, I've cut 55-gallon drums that way, right in half!
Used 'em for geranium planters in the front yard."
"Well thanks, Fred, I'll give it a try."
I skipped out of there with nothing to buy!
So I tried it, my saw screaming eeyow, eeyow, eeyow
going over the corrugations, the sparks shooting
and the steel glowing on the cut. I could see Fred
bent half-around a barrel, his muscles steady
in that ungodly noise. Well hell, I thought, successful
and deaf, wearing my roofer's hat.
You gave me a new combination, Fred,
nothing wrong with that.

ADDITION

We walked across the lawn that was once
a grain field to the fieldstone house
I used to play in, where box elders grew
among plaster, old canning jars, and crumbling
harness gear—the shell
rebuilt now
as my father's house.

He showed me how he was facing
the added wing with stones he had gathered
from the fence rows: with more care
than the homesteaders once took
in burying granite and limestone whole
in those thick walls, he placed
a black gneiss so the grain was right,
hefted the sledge, and swung, his motion
stiffer, his face more lined than I remembered.
He touched the opened, glittering halves
with his calloused thumb
and told me he like finding the hidden patterns.

I see him on the fence-rows I used to hike along,
between fields he used to farm:
he pulls stones out of wild raspberry
and flaking barbed wire tangles,
lifts them into the Ford pickup—or
he rests in the shade of scrub trees,
judging how much more weight
the squat tires can bear.

Once we sat on the stones, resting
next to rows of oats we had cut and shocked.
There was the sun and the sweat,
the elm trees were still living, rustling;
we sat, the future working inside me,
my father picking at yellow stubble,
as if by that he could hold off
the auction that was sure to come.

We never talked much. But his placing
of stone to stone, his opening
the seals of the earth,
tells me I must join word to word,
deed to deed,
live worthy of my father's house.

INSUFFICIENT LIGHT

He thought it was a perfect shot,
her shy face above the icing.
But the Colorburst feeds him a blank
that clouds to blue-black.

Maybe the pall is domesticity—
gold-white spots burning in—
She appears in silhouette,
before a window with unearthly trees.

Light infidelities.
He can just make out her dark smile,
then looks up at her.
Development starts.

SCENES OF GREEN LIGHT

i

My brother stared through the tractor exhaust
at the rippling land and the trembling clouds
as he drove us out to the field. My father
stood on the drawbar, narrowing his eyes against
the cigarette that seemed to cut furrows in his face
as he looked to where the windows were strung
like fat cables on the east slope. I stood
in the wagon, my knees bent to take its lurching,
my hands firm on the creaking endgate.
The hay-sling rope felt hard as a bead of weld
under my ankle-high workshoes. In the fence-row
tangled with brush and barbed-wire, bleached posts
slanted where they rotted, jutting out of fieldstone
once hauled by horses with the stoneboat made of
rough planks and strap iron we scrapped that year.

ii

We were the burning end of the slow fuse, the windrow.
The steady pulling haunted my brother's daydream.
The stubble popped against the tires and the smell
of cured hay was dense as smoke. Brittle leaves flaked
like ashes and fell in our collars as the hayloader's
tine-studded hardwood arms pushed up the alfalfa
ribbon my father caught and pitched to where
I clambered as the wagon slanted and shifted.
He called for help, it was so thick on the low side
of the hill; together we sank our forks and pulled.
He gasped as the clot gave way; I flushed
with a new heat as he called me strong.

The sling-load of hay, long stems streaming back,
soared to the half-full mow, the carrier clicking
on the hangars my father nailed to the peak of the roof.
I pulled the trip-rope; the sling burst open,
the load fell with a dry, rushing sound,
puffing leaves that drifted down as we climbed
the ladder. The hard, worn ridges of the axe-trimmed rungs
stung my yellowed callouses. I stalled on the oak
cross-beam, crouching in the hot, still air,
and then jumped into the mow so the dust churned and glowed
in slits of light. I tugged against a knot of hay;
my father showed me how to pull apart the layers
which caught the light in green flashes
as he pitched them against the wall. I saw
the yellow spiders retreat in quivering webs
and the green light darken in mazes of stems and leaves.

THE POWER OF THE DOE

i

Think of it as a film run backwards:
condensing clouds of dust, the game warden's car
moves in reverse on our valley road,
guided by the doe's glazed eyes.

ii

The warden's hands seem to follow the rope
that unties her from the trunk.
She pulls him by the hand with her hind leg,
slithers across the grass,
feeling the way with her tongue.

iii

We who were already forgetting
step back as in a hesitant dance,
in light no longer failing,
to the place where blood gathers.

iv

You and I in hunted love
see the deer begin to twitch.
Our daughter of seventeen, never so far,
has come so close to watch.

v

Blood flows up the tawn coat
into the waiting skull.
Doe hairs cling to my damp clothes.
We exchange a look,
finality draining into shock.

Laura backs to where the others stare.
The silence fades into crescendoes of echo
as the reflexes sharpen to total spasm,
gunshot birth.

The warden aiming received the bullet.
He holsters his gun
and with his palm face out
warns the children to come.

They come snowballing hope.
He strokes the paralyzed flank,
touches the scab that creases the spine,
explains like a shaman in his reversed tongue.

The does slides up to my sagging embrace.
It's a long climb to the high field.
We're chilled and wet; you prop my arm.
We'll stop at the stream.

Her black hooves, layered with white,
are couched on watercress.
She won't drink.
You raise her white-whiskered mouth.

The water erupts, sprays us
on its way to her. She's getting strength in those
two good legs
that churn against my grasp—
we can even laugh.

xii

Our grotesque baby. I'm holding her
belly up, her long legs sticking out all over.
She's wide-eyed, the lashes long and curved,
the ears laid low. There's rough footing
on these ridges. A stray dog circles and snaps.

xiii

The house, the yard, the children there
getting just a little younger, grow small.
My arms strain to keep her, but she's
getting lighter, the curve of her spine
rising in the hoop of my arms.

xiv

We rest among rock and sod,
oak and birch.
The doe is calm, certain, intent.
She turns to watch the dog.
We could be content.

xv

In the last ravine she squirms, writhes,
wrenches out of my grip down to flat rock.
I hear the hooves of a great avenging buck—
it's her heart—beating primal terror!

xvi

I seize her, clamp the oval of her chest.
Her front legs flail, spittle froths her mouth—
she bellows, arching her neck, cries so hoarse,
so deep, greater than my rage to possess—
she drags me, staggering, clinging into the brush.

She releases me.
I step back to where
decision softens, the letting go,
our voices fingering new words.

Our hands join.
We move among blueberry, honeysuckle,
under hickory whose leaves shine
the afternoon's climbing light.

The doe waits for days in that quiet
and then lifts, twisting, soaring,
to the high field where she incants
a sliding, leaping dance.

The charmed bullet unearths
and sings to splice the severed nerve,
to mate with its shell of brass—
the hunter recoils amazed.

Think of it as the last, frozen frame,
or even a picture on an urn:
you and I hiking toward morning,
remembering the blood, the cry, the quiet.

Beryle Williams

GOODBYE AT THE GULF

Kissing her
carefully, we allow
only our children's young lips
to sink dangerously deep
in the fragrant crushed velvet
of my mother's cheeks

pack in the fruit
pecans and preserves
and shells gathered together
on their warm winter shores

touch once more
gently
my eighty year old
farmer—father's hands
gone soft as a child's

a fragility encountered
in the spaces
behind eyes
in the heart

anticipated
in the distance
between this place
and where we are going

propelling us northward
away from them, away from them
blindly
through a blizzard
through a rage
of love

toward our own winter

BRIDGE CROSSED

I wonder if this old bridge
has ever known
lovers beneath, in shadow
lying close and damp
on grassy slope
after swimming in deep water.

POSTCARD HOME

My Love

   This is just a note to say
I'm on my way home
at least my thoughts
are aimed that way
but I should warn you

this is an old and winding road
with branches like crooked
beckoning fingers
leading off to somewhere else
or nowhere . . . take care

               my love

FOR A GLIMPSE OF NIGHT-FALL ON WATER

Slowly and quietly, the way dusk
in late summer forest demands,
we come down from our high camp

and cautious, but less tentative
than ourselves,
near the edge of the darkening lake
are two small fawn.

We grow more silent
and heavier by the hour; we stumble
and grumble inwardly more, both turning
fifty this year, our eyes
giving less value back for the effort

but wrapped now
in the sudden gift of this vision
we become light, touching each other
more gently than the stilled, soft air
that surrounds us. We see

this browsing pair, reflections
of the white stems of trees and the last
dusk-fringed clouds so clearly
that night may never fall.

We move softly
around the shore's curve toward them,
our steps, lighter than they have been
for years, scarcely bending
a blade of grass.

On a small hill of fern, we pause,
every slight movement we make in rhythm
with leaves and waves lapping near us

even the brushing away
of a mosquito, a delicate wand-wave
of finger, our breathing, without effort

suspended as we watch, in fear
the fawns may suddenly look up
startling us both
back to our nests in deep woods.

TEA BREAK

On my Celestial Seasonings
Mandarin Orange Spice
herb tea   No Caffeine   envelope
with only one bag left
I just read
"The work of the world does not wait to be
done by perfect people"
and all this time
I thought I had to do it all.

THE WOLVES

They are there again tonight
ahead, at the bend in the road,
their shapes the dark ground
of a ritual I cannot explain

the proud silver-gray, the mottled
other, and at the lead, as always
the strange and powerful black
gleaming like onyx

their eyes catching cold fire
in the beam of my lights
as I swing into the curve
that will turn me away from them.

Again, I brake almost
to a stop, again almost
step out of my car
instinctively, the way bodies

slip out of cocoons
or skin, but something—
their stillness—stops me,
that is, keeps me moving

through the frozen night,
remembering it is always winter
when I see them, always
this stark back-drop of snow.

Yet I know they must be there
in all seasons, moving higher along
the hill, perhaps watching among pines
until some sign calls them down

to this bend, bright eyes dimming
as I spin away, breaking trail
through drifts of their silence
and this terrible urge to stop.

THE TWIN CITIES

"Say city," he demands
"say city in your poem.
This is where you live now.
Take hold of the square-cornered forms
that wall your neighbors' lives,
the phallic shafts of steel and glass
coupling with smog to block the sun
from shrinking city parks.

"Carve your words
in city cement, not mountain rock.
Follow the street walker, not
the screech owl; record the babbling
of winos on Hennepin Avenue, not
the loons on Lost Lake.

"Your farm past is past. Let it be.
Touch me," he begs, "I am City.
I am real. Your nature is a dream
you escape to from eyes in dark doorways,
flash of the knife under streetlamps,
screams of raped women, of children
abandoned in cold rooms, or lost
in their own heads. Men
going mad in buses, subways, cars
in the eternal high-speed drive
to make it.

"Come to terms with, speak out of
where you live."

With his passion for this moment,
for the carved, sheer instant
that begs the leap, making
a blast furnace of his eyes
near mine, how can I tell him
after so many years of sharing
city friends, shapes and streets,
that as we grow older, my poem,

like my body, rejects unnatural substance,
aborts the alien forms, and I have
never lived in his city.

OLD SHOES VIEWED FROM THE BATHTUB

If I just leave them sitting there,
the old black and white saddle-shoes
I've owned so long they must feel
they own me . . . if I just leave them
where I stepped out of them
on the deep blue bathroom rug
they might never move
from that spot. I think no one
would ever pick them up

except as I am now, suspending them
in the abstract space of mind
because they remind me of a painting
I saw once of an old shoe, or
maybe I sketched it myself, or
is it the drawing by my son
I'm remembering? But suppose

they just stayed there forever
with no one wanting or perhaps
daring to touch them, not
just because they're old enough
to crumble in their hands but
because they are so distinctly
mine, especially the left one
with a hole in the toe
where my left big toe must turn
slightly upward and the worn place
on the outside of the foot
where it's widest. Maybe I'm

heavier on that side, my
heart, or with one hip higher
I walk with a limp, some
lop-sided stress no one knew I had,
not even me. But
oddly enough, it's the right one
whose black saddle is more worn
. . . does the left one often
sit on the right one, I wonder? Do
I? One tongue is crooked, one
torn out. What do they do to each other
or themselves with me in them?

They've held their sides firm and high
and their arches aren't broken
but why haven't I noticed
they're both somewhat down at the heel
at odd angles that appear
they're tilting apart from one another?

Say I leave and they just stand there
forever holding some essence
none of us were aware of, and friends
or strangers passing the doorway,
prospective buyers, perhaps,
or just visiting, look in . . .

say the old house has turned into
a museum . . . say I got famous after all
and the old pair of shoes have become
a museum piece, themselves, like
"This is the bed she slept in . . .
this is the chair where she sat
to write" and "These are the shoes
she wore, just as she left them" . . .
would anyone see me in them, see

better who I was by them, want to
try them on for size, would my children
grow embarrassed, finally carry them
back to my closet? Should I?

Susan Firer

SLOW FALLING FROM SNOW

in that slow falling from snow
i took three to juggle
a glass apple
a fish's heart
& a blond child's ballet

in the deep starred night
how pretty
by candle light
the circle they make
the pink slipper's ribbons
following the small stemmed
glass apple the fish's heart

we all make our own magic
choose our own objects
decide the time we'll give or take
watch me
here, now, i am practicing

can you see it this time
my practicings so slow
i become a painting
the objects circling my face
a halo
a portrait
only the ribbons on the slippers
tangle in my voice

EGG SHELLS AND ICE STORMS

First the birds came like a weather
front thick and fast filling
trees with nests and eggs.
Then the winds came winds
that kept the windows clattering
and knocking day and night nervous hard winds
so hard they took the water right out of the riverbed.

The morning after things quieted down
we went out. The grass was light
blue everywhere we walked birds' eggs
small & delicate, whole & shattered. The sound
our feet made walking the blue landscape
was more fragile than the sound of walking
on black beetles on hot summer nights.

The sound was more like the first catch
in a mother's breath when she finds out
her favorite child has died before her.
Or like that funny early spring in Indiana,
when the rains fell then froze. Late afternoon
the winds knocked the ice covered branches together.
Everywhere all night the sounds the shattering
the shattering, breaking and falling;

and I felt the whole state would have to be different
after that night-after that blue egg shell morning.
But the good neighbors shoveled and swept
trying to clean up like after a war,
or a marriage, or a generation
all that fussing to hurry back to what
is hardly ever realized in the first place.

THE FETISH BOX OF EYE & SUN

the sunlight falls in great chunks
through the skylight
in the natatorium roof, under water i
watch the other bodies swim through it.
bodies lovely in the distortion
of water & sunlight falling sunlight
holding water, shining & moving bodies.

a body halo that seems right, as if
our bodies should always shine
just that way. i recognize that light
it rose from a painting we looked
at late one night in bed the japanese
painting more than a night's light

set in an early morning japanese garden
three people:
the man leans back on a ledge
his robe pulled up over his belly
his penis long waiting for the lady
sitting on an emerald green silk
scarf swing, the scarf is tied
to a flowering tree branch & she
sits naked & glowing legs wrapped
wide around the silk swing.
a second lady pushes her
gently onto the waiting man.

there are lights & there are lights
but there is no power in the shadows
when loveliness lets loose
beyond all possible expectations.

LEARNING SEX FROM THE DICTIONARY

I
1961
trembling, I read it
brazier-b-r-a-z-i-e-r
noun: a vessel holding burning coals (as for heating)
yikes
what was going to happen to my tits
when i grew older
that they would need a brazier

II
1962
when I asked my mother
when would i get a period like my sisters
she said, "when you start
high school
i said
"the first day,
when you put your foot on the step
or
when you go in the door"
i was not kidding
she said,
"go to your room"
she was not kidding either

III
1965
a junior in high school & what
the teachers called too socially orientated
i left my books in my locker at school
& did not listen
to the news or read newspapers
except to try & find out what rape meant.
secretly, i had looked the word up
in my pocket book merriam-webster
it said
rape-to commit rape on: ravish

so i looked up ravish
it said
1) to carry away by violence
2) to overcome with emotion
   & esp. with joy or delight

i read the newspapers to try & find out
if rape was ravish 1 or ravish 2
but i kept getting rape confused with rap
& only found out about politicians criticizing one another

i confided
my confusion
about rape to Linda Horwitz
(her father was a doctor—
& had many books—
she knew it all!)

she showed me one of the books
it had a picture of a man's
penis in it, the first penis i ever saw

under the picture it said
elephantiasis of the penis

that was rape she said

i knew then
rape was ravish 1
no doubt
rape was ravish 1

THE SECRET

the first night i remember
waking to him
he was standing in the doorway
holding an indian sword
red sash across his bare chest
nothing else on
neither of us mentioned it

another night
he was a one man band
the large bass drum balanced
on his bare stomach
cymbals where his pants
rubbed off the leg hair
harmonicas horns washboards & kazoos

a one man band he stood
silent 2:45 a.m.
after that i hid
the wedding pictures

what is he
on nights i sleep through

the minister has told me
he has seen him in the early
morning in the church courtyard
stroking the doves
at st. francis' feet
laughing & rolling
in the wet grass

believe you me
in the street light
in the moon light
in this house's windows
in the urgency of morning
we learn to take

our hearts in hand
like clocks set them
forward or backward
depending on the time & season

THIS WINTER OF THE RAIN OF GEESE

The snows had all
melted and run off in a bewildering
week and a half February thaw.
The hunters' black lead shot
lay on the marshes and the bare
farmers' fields. The Canadian
geese mistook the lead shot for seed.
Now farmers' acres are covered
with thousands of rounded bellies-
dead geese. Years before
I had worked in the Horicon
marsh lands and listened
to farm kids talk revenge
on the birds that fed on
their fathers' fields.
No one then could have imagined
anything this awful
marshes and fields acres
carpeted with the silenced wings
and bodies of the beautiful Canadian geese.
Awful
how a politician's signature or
a hunter's choice of shot
could quiet, empty the sounds
and shadows from the Mississippi Flyway.

FOOTSTEPS

Jim, you & i are the bear & the ox
drawing the wagon

in Bobbio it can be seen in bas-relief
carved in 1480

there
it commemorates Columban
the Irish saint
"who ordered the bear
that killed one of the oxen
dragging stones for his church
to take the victim's place"

Columban
the wandering saint
whose footsteps
were said to fill with *Leguminosae*
(a pretty & useful plant of the pea family)

our footsteps fill with words & children
at times the wheels on our wagon break

Edward Armstrong asks an interesting question
when he writes about nature's mystics
"who among us is entitled to judge
between saints"

not me
i am the ox
i ask this question
if we could choose
what our footsteps would fill with
what would be your choice

THE WOMAN FROM MATTOON

When Ruby blew into town,
mothers bought their sons
one-way Trailway tickets;
wives took their husbands to Oshkosh,
"Lake Winnebago is so
interesting this time of the year."

Ruby Montanna was ruinous.
Anybody who wanted to
knew that. When she got through
with a man, he was marked
up like a drunk and determined
sailor who feels nostalgic
& visits a Great Lakes Tattoo Parlor
at 2 a.m.

Ruby often said, "I hate everything—
everything. If I find a record I like
I buy it & play it 'til I hate it.
If I find a man I like I take him
home 'til I hate him.
I hate everything."

I rode behind Ruby
on The City of New Orleans
spring of '82.
Before we pulled out of town
8 empty Dixie cans
came rolling under her seat toward me.

With eyes of hand drawn glass
she shouted at the young good looking
man who was sitting alone
a few seats kiddy corner from us,
"Hey, you need a partner?
I need a partner."

39 Dixies later
small towns were lighted announced
by Ruby's remarks:
Jackson, Mississippi—"Lady,
give that kid some tit
so's we can all get some quiet."

(The next remarks were addressed to
the young good looking man who was
by that time sitting beneath her)
Memphis—"That's one classey hard on,
honey"

Paducah—"How'd you like a mess of this?"

Neoga—"Come on sweetie get off in
Matoon with me. Call your girlfriend
tell her you're held up 'til tomorrow.
I'll make you a morning of peter pancakes
and an afternoon of bliss."

4 a.m.
Mattoon
& that guy she picked up stumbling
behind Ruby. Him trying to juggle
his luggage & his drunk,
trying hard to catch up.

In the spring trains of the night's south
Ruby, as always, was a natural disaster.
Made you feel like the Red Cross following her
those damaged bodies thrown everywhere behind her.

Andrea Musher

TELLING THE DIFFERENCE

I begin my journeys north in autumn
the field ditches are brittle with gold stalks
and turned over patches of earth muzzle up
rich black to the light
bold before the snow
At the marsh—the wild-life preserve—the Canadian geese
are circling and settling
small groups detaching themselves
from the littered hordes to form
the ragged V they will pull southward
raveling and unraveling in the sky
like beginner's knitting
their cries waking me from the drowse
of driving
begging what is bunched in me
to beat
upward/ upwind stretching
as I pass through the town of Eden
two bars and a trailer park
on the way to the prison
that nestles under a ridge of woods
scorched with fire colors
and apple trees still yielding
fruit

I could be a guard
I could be an inmate
I could be a woman just hired to teach classes
there's no way to tell
the difference
this could be a finishing school for girls
(and it is)

they complain about the starchy foods

and their lives
badly knit to begin with
unravel here

the Warden wears her constant cigarette
her tailored 3-piece suit
and a heavy ring on every finger
for protection
her military jargon keeps sentiment
in the pit of her stomach
where her ulcer burns
reminding her that she too
is a woman trapped
by the power structures
she can't control
she lives like a target
answering her five different colored telephones

we arrive
where we flee
I swore I'd never teach high school
and this is the grand exaggeration
of hall passes and bells
that herd masses
endless nightmare of adolescence
I still awake sweating

today five pregnant prisoners are carving pumpkins
not a nonsense rhyme
an arbitrary act
in the Basic Skills Lab
they speak casually of the nurse's
nutritional pep talks
and I'm thinking of the centuries of women
who scraped out the extras
with knitting needles
they are allowed to hold
the newborn for five days
then they're locked back empty
breasts and stomachs drying hardening

they ask for certain simple things

toys for the children when they visit
but the trick of with-holding becomes a habit
for some who hold power
and even the toys can become a way to control
and it's not like you think
there's no way to tell the difference
you begin to wonder
why they have to stay
if you're free
to leave

they say you only stop "doing time"
when you're ready to stop doing time
like a drug like a home they return to this place
for weeks the geese seem innumerable
but by Christmas the marsh is frozen still
silent under a grey hammer sky
a partridge crosses my car's path
I shave past it and am arriving again
the tension tightening its noose
around my neck

it is said that the women disappoint time
and again
getting right back out hustling drugs
and their asses
forging checks to buy color t.v.s
that they sell to buy cocaine
that they sell to buy more cocaine
that they sell to buy color t.v.s

there's Fred the five foot cat burglar
in combat boots and tattoos
blonde hair greased back in a duck-tail
and t-shirt sleeves rolled up even on the coldest days
to display the bulge of small biceps

once they were taught to set the table
while wearing white gloves

there's Betsy who grew up starving

in the 13 child sharecrop family in Mississippi
her teeth falling out as her breasts grew in
and Smolina with the small slice out of her left ear
where she wears three gold pirate rings
who murdered her pimp
and who's now the Daddy of her own harem

and yes they touch themselves and each other
for pleasure and power
manipulating in small measure

there's not enough snow this year
and the landscape stands bald and shiny
bones for the wind to gnaw
iron teeth holding us all locked inside ourselves
and of course I've told it all wrong
exaggerating the extremes the picturesque
when there's no way to tell it
they could all be you

I preach thesis paragraph topic sentence
form and order
as always the bars are a grid laid on the mind
the jello mold that will make the wavering
gluey mass of self stand frilled and shaped at the table
of predatory hands and mouths
—all the better to eat you with my dears—

the wolf's intestines are the passages we live in
each chemical convulsion washing over us
breaking us down
as we cling to the tubular walls
or wash through to the bowels
and this is how we are pressed into waste

the farmers fear the lack of snow cover
its seep and melt so necessary to seed life
and the cold's blue blade
lodged in the heart
makes drawing breath harsh
as the geese come straggling back to the ragged fields

and on the prison grounds they have raked up an acre of earth
burning it raw
not for planting
but for more segregation cells and treatment rooms

now in April with tulip tips pushing up
and lilac buds studding thin limbs
the snow comes
a blizzard of despair
piling our griefs in white public places
the heart clutches this new wound
like a lost child
and the geese huddle stranded
a flurry of wings on the frozen waters
blurring like over-exposed film

MY MOTHER INFORMS ME
THAT SHE IS GOING TO HAVE A FACELIFT

She says she hates her wrinkles/ that she thinks Phyllis
Diller looks beautiful. And I feel that I'm losing control
of her life. I haven't raised her
consciousness so I could suffer such an ungrateful turn
of events. I ask what her friend, Rita, thinks—
remembering too late that Rita won't even answer the phone
without her make-up on. And my mother
points out that it's a woman's right
to choose the newest improvements in medical technology
(But how am I to come to terms with my aging/ if she changes
the face that was mine from the start?)

There is no dissuading her so I compose the following poem:

In Praise of Wrinkles
Or a Plea Against My Mother's Intended Facelift

Let me speak of the eyes' blue fire
banked in filigree
burning true to the heart

or of sacred linen garments stitched
in finest gold thread
and of maps whose creases yield
islands of light

There are nets to be woven in an ever
more intricate mesh
and a great casting out upon the waters
to steal the pattern of the tides
the waxing and waning of the moon
tolling in one face

I tell you there is radiance in
the unpleating smile riding its ripples
outward to the dark shore
where the wise ones gather
the lifelines we need

and I think: What of me?
arranging and re-arranging a scattering of lines
on a page/ as if I could find my true face
but it's always in the next poem
wearing less wrinkles, a nicer haircut, leading
a more significant if not more elegant life

Love would come easily to such a face/ such a poem
would invite feast and celebration without guilt or fat
would have acclaim, a country house and invitations
to visit China   such a face/ such a song would grow younger
stretching into the light of the longest days, planting flowers
gathering guests and verses that mingle life and death
in the perfect friendship that would transform and charm
all our days to come

VACATION POST CARDS FROM THE EAST COAST

In D.C. I jogged through the cherry blossoms
spring spangles
dangled there
on an intake of breath

In Boston I watched the marathon runners come in
pumping proud-breasted
at the digital finish
stumbling later/ blood stains
on t-shirts where nipples bled
feet full of sores
walking back and forth in tin foil mantles
silver sheets handed out to hold body heat in
the first 6 hundred finishers eat free Columbo yogurt
and the Queen does not sweat
Rosie Cruz in her laurel wreath
walks suspect
no other runner saw her
pass
no knowledge of her
at the checkpoints

In Washington the President dedicates the Frances Perkins Bldg.
and the fastest stamp on record is peeled
off the presses to commemorate
the woman in the hamburger hat
Madame Secretary who would retreat
to be among the Silent Sisters after fighting
for Social Security, Unemployment Compensation, Minimum Wage
and Job Safety Standards
A stone elephant will stand holding up
her name
Some people will have envelopes with her picture
bearing the wavy semaphor of cancellation

In New York the streets buzz my feet
I lick up shop windows
shiny as sugar pastry and patent pumps
The women lovers feeding me croissants and wine tell me:

"—the baby's two—she calls us both, 'mother'"

If I had a child
the things I would do
the things I couldn't do
pasting down thoughts like postage stamps
feeling my life blur
needing the zipcode of family
for safe delivery

The Washington cherry blossoms are specially bred
to bear no fruit
white flames burst from pink buds
promise nothing
but the moment

They claim that Rosie Cruz leapt out of the sidelines
They ask her:
         do you remember the other runners?
         the landmarks?
She says: I don't remember anything
         the past is a blur
         I am here now
         arriving arriving
they have uncovered evidence of brain surgery
on two occasions
the tricks the mind plays

At lunch in New York future mothers discuss methods
"I don't want to do the turkey baster thing. I want to know the father."
"—Biblicly? He's just a sperm donor."
"He's a genetic inheritance."
We carry our past for centuries
mutating slowly
we collect coded cells
passing messages

I hear that Rosie has lost her wreath
and the marathon monitors promise
stricter surveillance in future
claiming that the revered old race
has lost its innocence

Bonnie Fisher

SOMETHING TO SAY TO YOU

My husband steps out of the shower, asks me why there
are blue spots on his undershorts. We are going
dancing. "I take no responsibility for the spots on
your undershorts," I tell him. "I'm not the CHEERY
lady of the wide screen TV who takes pride in the
sun pure whiteness of her husband's undershorts."
"Well," he says, "I know how the spots got on my
undershorts. It was when you were gone. George
asked the kids to wash his new blue Datsun and they
wiped it with my undershorts." "WHEN I WAS GONE?"
I yell. "WHEN I WAS GONE?" "I don't like this
conversation," he says. "Why did you start it then?"
I snap. "I just wanted to have something to say to you,"
my husband answers. And then we go dancing.

OLD MOVIES

On the lake snow swirls. Seven foot drifts block our doors. Lights from fishhouses flicker but even with our three-quarter ton plow, we can't get out to them. Like Whittier, we are snowbound.

"Let's look at all the old movies," we always say. At last there is time.

We bundle up in flannel nightgowns, wrap ourselves in comforters, pass the popcorn round. Lights out. Projector on.

There we are at Niagara Falls. The kids are sticky with cotton candy. "Say cheese," we all say.

There's Daddy, patched army slacks, stick in his hair, raking leaves in neat piles, Nan and me rolling in the leaves, tossing them in the air, Mama, young-eyed, carrying wieners, relishes, roasting sticks, mouthing, "Stop that now."

There's Benny taking his first step.

Grandma kissing all the grandbabies, Grandma bearing in the golden Christmas turkey, Grandma and me buttoning the little dolls into miniature sweaters. Grandma, cheeks flushed, dark hair curling over heavy eyebrows, fingernails painted poinsettia red, wearing rings, rings.

The kids squirm. They clamor. "Let's look at the movies backwards now."

There's Benny taking his first step, backwards. Nan walking out of the church on her wedding day, backwards. Grandpa running backwards out of the park his arms outstretched to catch us, Nan and me running backwards hollering just out of his grasp.

We slap our thighs, clap our hands, the kids roll around the carpet. This is so hilarious.

Niagara Falls gushes up out of the gorge, rolls over the rocks, backs into the placid river like a mad dog sucking in its froth, quieting, calming, becoming the family puppy again.

There's Benny. Lou is hosing icecream off of him. He is madder than hell. The water goes back in the hose. The icecream comes off the washcloth and messes Benny up. He backs over to the driveway where the cats are lapping up his icecream. The cats back off. The icecream rises magically from the ground, floats magically into his hand. Benny looks surprised, then full of joy, as if we never will find him floating face down in the Apple River.

Projector off. Popcorn bowls to the sink. Kids to bed. Curled in darkness, I dream.

We clutch each other in the mist over the Niagara. I can't see your face. Are you my mother? Are you my sister? Are you my sister's child?

You slip out of my arms, slide into the river, spill over the Falls.

I see my grandmother in the mist, white veils blooming, it is her honeymoon, goats still gracing riverbanks. "Grandma," I call. She doesn't hear me.

She is 93. We are in the nursing home. I smooth Vaseline over her lips, spoon icechips into her mouth, comb her hair back from her face as I have my babies' hair. Her fingers flicker against my palm and she dies.

In a pew in Barron, Wisconsin, my aunt and I count hymnals, we count veils. But even with our eyes closed we see the tiny coffin.

All the mothers become one mother. All the sisters become one sister. All the children become my child and I slip over the Falls.

There we are, Karen and me. She is stuffing peppers into steaming jars. I am reading her my poems. She doesn't say a word but comes, puts her arms around me, kisses me. I don't know what to say. I move away. This is all wrong.

Running it backwards doesn't make it better. Backwards or forwards, one of us is moving away.

The ice booms. Bedsprings creak. I wake up, check the kids, make coffee, let it get cold.

It's too late to call you but I go to the phone anyway, dial, wait. "How's the weather there?" I'll ask. "Good, how's it there?" You'll say. "Blizzard here, How're the kids?" "Crabby as hell, How're you?" "I love you." Static on the line, always static. "I love you," I'll say.

The operator comes on. "Sorry lines down due to blizzards throughout Minnesota this call cannot be completed please try again."

I hang up, make more coffee, get the comforter Grandma made, pull it around me, watch the lake.

The wind whines in the TV antenna, howls in the pipes, cries in the eaves. I sip my coffee. Maybe I will try again.

WAITING

The lake is still glass eye.
Trucks haul fish houses
creaking and clanging onto the ice.
Red-jowled men hammer license tags
over doorways, thread barbed hooks
through minnows' eyes, pass
the whiskey round.

Beneath the surface, walleye swim slow.
I slip with them naked over rock ledges,
lose myself in webs of decaying weeds,
have no breath, no heartbeat,
roll like a pebble on currents of dream.

I am fish now,
a useless glazed eye,
finding my way with my body now,
feeling between dock posts with my fins.
I am formless, waiting.
My hair floats round me like eelgrass.

GOING TO THE DANCE

1. The Godmother

She sits
at her desk
her crinkly hair
spread round her
like a fan.

I tell her
what I've never
told anybody

how much
I crave dancing.

"What will you give
to go dancing?"

She asks almost without breathing
almost without moving her lips
without stirring a single silver hair.

"All I have
anything
all I am
everything."

"It will mean,"

she says,
shaking her head slightly,

"giving up everything."

2. The Dress

She gives me a dress
the color of hibiscus.
The dress is full of wrinkles.
I press and press
but I can't get out the wrinkles.

I put it on anyway,
start for the dance
wearing wrinkles.

3. Tangles

I waltz toward the music
of fiddles and accordians.

The straps holding up my dress
break. My shoes come untied.
I get twisted in the straps,
turned around, tangled.

The dancing
the dancing.

When will I get to the dancing?

FARA

1. When I First Met Fara & Her Family

At recess she clung to the cyclone fence
at the edge of the playyard. In class
she seldom spoke, seldom looked up
from her books.

I followed her home
where her family, shy as moths,
hovered behind the porch screen.

I waited on her steps five days
until they recognized me as one
of their own and invited me in.

Their house was airless.
Dark damask curtains kept out light.
They huddled together
and bloomed in each other's presence
like mushrooms in a cave.

Four of them slept in the single bedroom.
Fara slept on the livingroom couch
next to the upright piano with the lid
pulled down tight over the keys.

After they had known me a while
they opened
the piano and asked me to play.

2. Fara Loves Me

High in the house
where pine eaves

cross over me
like church steeples,

I wait for Mama to call me.

Her silky hand
reaches me
under the cover.

Mama?

No, it's Fara
slipping into the sheets,
Fara sliding her hand over my hip,
Fara kissing my warming mouth,
Fara clutching me deep in her soft arms.

A foot falls on the attic step.
A shadow blocks the light filtering
through the irregular threads
of my comforter.

This time Mama has come.

This time Mama has come to call me out.

3. Fara Has Been Taken Away

Fara has been taken to an empty house
at the edge of the river.
I hurry there looking for her,
knowing as I see the broken windows,
she will not be there.

Three faceless boys pursue me.

"There's quicksand in the river,"
they hum,

"you'll never get away."

I hurl myself over the riverbank,
struggle toward the opposite shore.
The current is stong and I am weak.
I remember the words of my Red Cross
swimming teacher:

"The only way to save yourself
is not to fight at all."

I turn on my back
and ride the swells
of the churning river.

4. What They Really Want

I cling to a sliver
of scaffolding
under the rose window
of St. Mary's Basilica.

Beneath me in the street
Fara and her family
chant my name.

I stretch my arms for balance.
Breeze billows my hair.
I want more than anything
to go down to them.

Behind me someone calls out,
I think it's my friend, Margaret.
"Are you awake?" She whispers.
"Are you wake?"

I open my eyes.
In the street below

cars line up waiting
for the traffic lights to change.

Fara and her family have gone.

5. What She Always Wants

I step into the elevator.
Fara is huddled in the corner.
Like me, she is grown-up now,
though she dresses as we did
when we were children.

Gradually I notice there are no
buttons in this elevator for
selecting a place to get off.
Fara turns slowly.
Even before she turns
I know there is no face
inside her knitted hood.

This elevator drops rapidly.
Like the one at the Hilton
it is all glass
and you can see
the shaft
as you go down.

Silt
then clay
with little shells
of insects and animals
trapped here,
tree roots reaching
downward into first
layers of rock.

We plummet to the water table,
hurtle past fault lines
are immersed in a terra cotta sea,
terrible fish cavorting,
bone men walking
without surfaces.

Where are the buttons to press?

I grow weak.
Fara's face begins
to reconstruct beneath her hood.

She holds out her arms to me.
I remember we have been lovers before.

Elizabeth Ann Knight

DAKOTA HOMESTEAD, 1879

The day my mother lay,
giving birth again,
my smaller sister
Anna died.
Neighbors dressed her
for burial
in my Finnish doll's clothes.
And seeing things plainly,
talked among themselves:
"It's too bad Amanda,
the sickly one, didn't die."
Amanda, I tugged that doll—
some other thing now
without her clothes—
out on the prairie,
buried it.
I never said where
and nothing gives itself away here,
but I lived
to bear children. Tell
my story.

JOHN RUNK, PHOTOGRAPHS, 1912

I hang on the edge of a shallow boat,
feet deep-thrust into the river,
the body finder.
Everyone knows John Jeremy
can't swim and can't drown.
I am an ugly man
but slip otter smooth under water
of the St. Croix, Mississippi.
The photographer waited.
My eyes moved
during the time of the exposure
and I look crazy.
I should. I see under water.
A man born in Stillwater, Minnesota,
like the monarch butterfly migrating
to a plateau in central Mexico,
inherits certainty of place.
Swimmers hug shallow water, ropes.
A stone in the river
cries to be moved.
People struggle for tools of rescue.
I fall straight and sure
through the reflected stars
and bring up bodies.
Hands on shore receive them
like treasure.

JOURNEYS

The train slides across Saskatchewan
at night, under the moon
lakes are disks of light.
Fishermen and their children
have built fires
and hold up fish
to the passing train.
Mothers, living and dead, wave,
old men stop coughing
and hang onto life
at the sight,
fish shaking brightly
by moon fire light.

FOR MARGARET WHO LIVES IN CALIFORNIA

You see your first fireflies in Nebraska
and drive the easy, flat miles.
At the cemetery in Grand Island
you knock on the caretaker's door,
calling an old woman out of her kitchen.
She carries a silver fork from the meal
you disturbed.
You give your grandparents' names, and
the old woman waves her fork—Why,
I lived in your grandmother's boarding house.
What a good woman she was!
(Your mother kept that secret.)
Here, take this! this fork,
it was your grandma's.

The old woman's been waiting
for you Margaret,
all these years
guarding your grandmother,
her silver fork, the feast.

THE PRINTER'S DEVIL GRANDDAUGHTER SINGS

He said he had no bed,
slept on a shelf
hand-made in the closet.

In the print shop
I find
grandfather provided.
Presses put to bed under
clean rags,
rollers in a wooden box called
their cradle.
Quoins haven't rusted.
Alone I learn:
lock a chase tight,
wet
good paper from the shelf.
We work so intently
—it's all in the hands,
transforming paper's white field—
that we are overtaken
by night at the window
like an old man slipping
into poems, knocking
letters into place.

At night he sees a little girl
riding
a bear in his closet.
O sly Eliza
you are quick as a girl.

WORKING AT THE WINTER'S EDGE

We return home to our mother
and do the work of dead men
before winter.
With sickles we strike at
the year's growth
of tall grass and vines
by the lake behind the house,
and looking up, see suddenly
a deer swim to our shore.
Red sumac and saplings
crowd the bank,
stone steps heave up,
and although we hurry,
our path is unsure.
We can't get close to him.
Twenty years ago a deer
staggered over these stones,
getting the feel of ground again.
We children caught sight of him
rising from the lake,
antlers tearing the still surface,
throwing water in a fierce circle.
And without hands, we lifted,
awkward and difficult, the deer
from startled water.
Lifted him over stone walls,
over snow fences,
and staggered after.

TWO FOR MARY

I. A Sailor's Granddaughter

My mother's always
been afraid of summer storms.
Electricity snaps cat-like
through her.
She paces the glass porch,
watching lake water
bear storm
to the house.
And fastening windows,
doors,
she harbors us.

II. The Thief

After my father died,
my mother surely stole us back.
We three played hide and seek summer
evenings into night.
Her fierce love
brought us like deer to the back door.
She cooked gold,
fed us bear-fat
and we lay in our beds,
plundered stars shining.

Brother Benet Tvedten

THE CALLING OF CLARENCE

Clarence's mother screamed when she came home and found the strange looking people sitting in her living room. Clarence quickly ushered her into the kitchen. "There's nothing to be alarmed about," he said.

"They look like the K.K.K. They're wearing bed sheets. Who are they?"

"They're the Apostles of the Lord."

"A cult?"

"That's what some people would call them."

"Clarence, what are they doing here?"

"I invited them for supper."

She knew her husband would raise hell when he came home and saw Clarence's bearded and barefooted guests wearing robes made out of white bed sheets. Jake was already exasperated with Clarence because of the boy's futile efforts to find a religious community that would accept him as a member. "Forget about it," he kept telling Clarence. "Go out and find a job."

Clarence sat at home all day long reading the brochures he received in the mail every morning from the vocation directors of religious orders. Jake was angry with their pastor for having given Clarence a directory listing four hundred orders of religious men serving the Church in the United States and abroad. Jake said, "If he writes all those places, can you imagine how long he'll be under our feet? He'll be home waiting for mail from now until kingdom come."

Myra agreed that Clarence should leave home, but she was more sympathetic than her husband. "He's searching, Jake. It will take a while for him to find something."

"He won't find it in the house," Jake said.

When Clarence graduated from high school, he'd told his parents that he wanted to become a priest. After one semester at the diocesan seminary, the rector told Clarence that he'd never make it to the priesthood. "Your grades are poor. You'd better go home."

Jake said, "What do you mean you couldn't hack the schoolwork? Seminarians don't even have to learn Latin nowadays."

"I'm going to try the Brotherhood," Clarence said.

He was at the novitiate of the Salesian Brothers for two months. The novice master told him, "You'd better go home Clarence. Your piety is so different than ours. Frankly, you're too pious."

When they got the phone call to come after him, Jake said to Myra, "So, he's too stupid to be a priest and too holy to be a Brother. What's next?"

Myra had tried talking Clarence into enrolling at the vo-tec school. "Learn a trade, Clarence. Then you can find a good job, and maybe you'll meet a nice girl, marry her and raise a fine Christian family."

"No girl will ever fall for me," he said.

"Well, when your acne clears up, that will help matters." Myra wished that her son would go to a dermatologist. A nineteen year old shouldn't have such a pimply face. But she couldn't get him out of the house for an appointment with the doctor.

"I'm called by the Lord. I just know it," he said.

"So are lay people called by the Lord. Your father and I have vocations too."

"But I'm called to something special," he said.

Jake reminded him, "Many are called, but few are chosen. And, it's obvious you're not going to be chosen."

Clarence would write a letter of application to the vocation director whenever he found a religous community which appealed to him because of its attractive brochure. The reply was always the same. The order did not accept a candidate unless he had completed two years of college or had some experience in earning his own livelihood.

"That means you'd better look for a job right now," Jake said. "Having worked is a prerequisite for getting in."

"I don't believe all orders are like that," Clarence said. "There's got to be another one like the Salesians. They took me in."

"Not for long," Jake said.

"When our Lord called the apostles, he didn't ask for prerequisites," Clarence said. "He just told them to drop what they were doing and 'Come follow me.' "

"The point is, Clarence, they all left their jobs."

Myra took the hamburger out of the freezer and put it in the microwave. She'd said the young men could stay for supper, but she refused to allow them to spend the night. "We don't have enough beds for six people," she told Clarence.

"They can sleep on the floor," he said. "They're used to hardships, and they've got sleeping bags."

"No. Your father is going to be upset enough by their staying here for a meal. You shouldn't have let them in the house."

"They're holy people," Clarence said.

"They look a little odd to me. Now go in and keep your eye on them. They might steal something."

"Not the Apostles of the Lord."

Well, she thought, I have something to be grateful about. Clarence isn't like them. He isn't traipsing around the country barefooted and in a bed sheet. It seems that young people today either have no religion or an excessive amount of it.

Clarence came back to the kitchen and asked if the Apostles could wash their robes. "They don't have any other clothing. Just what's on their backs."

"No," she said. "There isn't time to wash and dry all those bed sheets before supper. And, they have to be out of here right after supper. Understand?" Their robes did need washing and so did they. Jake would have a fit sitting down to a meal with six men reeking of perspiration. "Maybe you should ask the guests to use the shower before your dad comes home."

Jake was surprised when Myra met him at the back door and told him there were six new guests for supper. "There are no cars out front," he said.

"No. They came by foot."

"From where?"

"I'm not sure."

"You're not sure? Myra, who the hell is in the living room?"

"Clarence invited them."

Clarence could see that his father was startled when he came into the living room. The Apostles, most of whom were sitting on the floor, stood up and waited to be introduced. "Dad, these are the Apostles of the Lord."

Jake, a confused look on his face, asked, "You mean Peter, Andrew, James, John and so forth?"

Clarence laughed. "No, Dad, not them. These guys call themselves the Apostles of the Lord because they're out preaching for the Lord."

"Is the Apostles of the Lord a religious order? One of those that you wrote to?"

"No. I didn't write them. They just showed up this afternoon when Mom was downtown."

Jake's face reddened. "By damn," he said, "you people belong to one of those cults."

"That's a word you people have applied to us," one of the Apostles said.

Clarence introduced the Apostle to his father. "Brother Isaac, this is my dad, Jake Kelly."

"Glad to meet you, Brother Jake."

"I am *Mister* Kelly."

"You are our bother in the Lord."

"Excuse me. I have to fix a drink." Jake went to the kitchen. He didn't say anything to Myra until after he'd got the Jack Daniels from the cupboard and slammed the door loud enough to make her jump. "What the hell is going on? Why are you cooking for them?"

"You're angry," she said. "I knew you'd be."

"What a sight to come home to."

"I know, but they've been on the road for days and they're hungry. They have to beg their food."

He went back to the living room with his drink. Stepping over the sleeping bag that was parked in front of his chair, he asked, grudgingly, "You fellows want a beer?"

"We don't use alcohol or drugs," Brother Isaac said.

"What about sex? Are you like Catholic monks?"

"We guard our members in sanctity and honor."

Jake laughed. "Oh, that's good. Guard your members."

Clarence said, "That's scripture, Dad. These guys can really quote scripture."

"What are they, Baptists?"

"No, Dad, they're the Apostles of the Lord. I told you that."

"I think you people are a bunch of freeloaders," Jake said to Brother Isaac. "Like somebody else I know." He looked at Clarence. "Why don't all of you go out and get yourselves a real job?"

"We are working for the kingdom," Brother Isaac replied.

The other Apostles expressed their assent. "Amen, amen Brother."

"You're a bunch of religious panhandlers," Jake said.

When Myra came to fetch them to the dining room, Brother Isaac said, "I thought I smelled meat frying. I hope we're not having meat."

"But we are," Myra said. "You can each have two hamburgers."

"We're vegetarians."

"Not tonight, boys," Jake said. "This lady has worked her butt off fixing supper for you."

Myra asked if one of the Apostles would like to say grace. Father Clarke, their pastor, always did when he dined with them. None of the Apostles volunteered. Jake waited, impatiently drumming his fingers on the table. He made the sign of the cross and muttered, "Bless us, O Lord, and these thy gifts."

Brother Isaac asked Jake, "Are you a good Catholic, Brother?"

"Yes I am, and don't call me Brother."

"Would you have eaten meat on a Friday in the old days?"

"Of course not."

"Then I hope you and Sister Myra will respect our wish to abstain from meat."

"Don't you think it's a bit rude, when you are a guest in someone's home, not to eat the food that is put before you?"

"Thou shalt not kill," Brother Isaac said. "That goes for taking the life of animals too. We cannot eat the flesh of God's creatures. We won't even wear shoes because they are made from the hides of slaughtered animals."

"I'll be damned," Jake said.

Myra picked up the salad bowl and went to the kitchen for more lettuce.

The table conversation was dominated by Jake and Brother Isaac. Myra fidgeted and wished that Jake didn't have to be so insulting. Clarence listened in awe as Brother Isaac explained the Apostles' way of life. The other Apostles spoke only to answer "Amen, amen Brother" to practically everything their leader said.

Myra asked the young man across the table from her what he had done before joining the Apostles of the Lord.

Brother said, "Brother Aaron was studying to be a chiropractor."

"How come he can't answer for himself?" Jake asked Brother Isaac.

"I am the spokesman for our group," he said.

"Amen, amen Brother," the other five Apostles said.

"Don't they ever get a chance to talk?"

"Of course they do. All of us are preachers."

They preached the release of Jesus from his captivity by the Churches. The Apostles of the Lord were founded by an evangelist named Liberator. He believed that people were not practicing authentic Christianity if they belonged to one of the organized religions. "Sectarianism is evil," Brother Isaac said. "It is a heresy which must be stamped out." Jesus came to establish the kingdom, not Churches. The hierarchies and ministers of the Churches prevent the establishment of the kingdom by identifying Jesus with their sects. "Jesus isn't a Congregationalist," Brother Isaac said.

"Jesus certainly isn't a Methodist," Brother Aaron said.

"Or a Lutheran," another Apostle said.

"Or Greek Orthodox."

Myra said, "Jesus is Jewish," but they ignored her.

"Or Presbyterian."

"Jesus isn't even Assembly of God."

Liberator commissioned his band of preachers to expose the heretics who teach falsely in Jesus's name. Brother Aaron said, "We must kick down the doors of the Churches so Jesus can be let out of his prison. So he can establish the kingdom."

Myra asked, "You mean kick down the doors in a figurative sense, don't you?"

Jake said, "They can't kick down any doors in their barefeet."

"Of course the Apostles of the Lord are despised by the clergy of the Churches," Brother Isaac said. "We expect that. Jesus was persecuted too by the high priests of his day."

Jake said, "We certainly haven't persecuted you. Taking you in, letting you use up all our hot water in the shower, giving you a meal which you won't eat."

Clarence was absorbing all this information about the Apostles of the Lord. He was reminded of the vocation literature he had received from the Dominicans. The Apostles of the Lord were so much like the Dominicans. St. Dominic had founded the Order of Preachers for the very same reason the Apostles of the Lord had come into existence. The Dominicans had preached against heresy. The Dominicans even wore white habits right up to the present time. Clarence had decided, after looking at all the vocation literature, that the Dominican habit was one of his favorites.

"I think we've been damn hospitable," Jake said as Myra went to the kitchen for another head of lettuce and to slice more tomatoes.

"The Lord bless you," Brother Isaac said.

"Are there any more of you Apostles in this neck of the woods?" Jake asked.

"No, but there are six hundred of us in the country and we're growing."

Clarence spoke for the first time during the meal. "How many did you begin with?" he asked.

"Just a few followers."

It was like that with the Dominicans, Clarence remembered from reading their history. St. Dominic started with six followers. By the time he died, there were thousands of Dominican friars all over the known world—preaching against heresy, saving souls.

When Myra returned from the kitchen, Jake said, "You fellows eat lettuce like rabbits." He thought of telling them that they looked like pigs. He wished that he'd made them take off their dirty bed sheets before coming to the table. "Don't you have any other clothes?" he asked.

"No," Brother Isaac said. "We are espoused to poverty. We own no buildings, no vehicles, no clothes other than the robes you see us wearing. Jesus told the people who were complaining about John the Baptist's appearance, 'Those who dress luxuriously are to be found in royal palaces.' Palaces like the Vatican."

"What do you mean by that?"

"You're a Catholic. You ought to know."

"You be careful. Don't go attacking my Church. I love it dearly."

"Your Church is ruled by the Antichrist."

"Watch it kid."

"You are married to the Whore of Babylon."

Jake banged his fist on the table and shouted, "That's it! Get out of my house. I'm not going to sit here and listen to you insult the pope and then my wife."

Myra said, "Oh, Jake, he didn't mean me. He meant the Church is the Whore of Babylon. Just settle down. We don't want to have a religious war."

"No! No! Get out of here. All of you."

"Calm down, Jake. I'll go get the dessert. Ice cream. Can you boys eat ice cream? It's a dairy product. Comes from cows."

Jake stood. Banging his fist on the table, he said, "Get! All of you. I'm going in the living room and I'm going to get your sleeping bags and toss them outdoors. And then I'm going to throw all of you out."

The Apostles of the Lord beat him to the living room. Brother Isaac, the last one to go out the front door, said to Jake, "We'll shake the dust from our feet and move on to another town. You won't listen to our message, but others will. Others will follow us."

Jake said, "Scram, buddy, or I'll call the police who will escort you out of town." He slammed the door shut and bolted it.

"Do you want another hamburger?" Myra asked when he returned to the dining room.

"No! I want to chew out Clarence for letting those punks in the house. Where is he?"

"I don't know."

"Clarence, are you in the toilet?"

"Maybe he went to his room," Myra said.

Jake went upstairs. "Myra, come here quick," he called, frantically.

When she got to Clarence's bedroom, she screamed for the second time that day. "Look at his bed!" It was stripped. The bedspread and pillow were on the floor. The sheets were gone. So was Clarence.

NOTES ON CONTRIBUTORS
AND ACKNOWLEDGEMENTS:

JAMES AGNEW (poems, p. 113) was born in Pittsburgh, Pennsylvania in 1958. He attended St. Edmund's Academy, Shady Side Academy, and Kenyon College. He presently lives in Minneapolis with his wife Robin, and his cat, Jane. He also writes short fiction.

CONSTANCE EGEMO (poems, p. 88) was a winner of the first Loft Mentor competition, has been published in several regional journals, magazines, and anthologies, and has given readings in the Twin Cities, Wisconsin, and California. She has taught poetry at the Loft. "Heartland" appeared first in *The Lake Street Review*.

RON ELLIS (poems, p. 221) teaches in an anonymous midwestern university, lives in a small patch of woods, meditates Quaker-Tantra, raises vegetables, and repairs Volkswagens. His poetry has appeared in *Commonweal*, *Strange Fruit 10*, *Wisconsin Poets' Calendar*, *New Jersey Poetry Journal*, *Poetry Northwest*, *The Pikestaff Forum*, *The Hika Bay Review*, *Poets On*, and others.

SUSAN FIRER (poems, p. 238) lives with her husband James Hazard and their children in Milwaukee, Wisconsin. Her first book of poems, *My Life with the Tsar and Other Poems*, was published by New Rivers in 1980. For the past three years she has been a lecturer at the University of Wisconsin-Milwaukee and more recently has been a member of The Great Lakes Poem Band. "The Fetish Box of Eye & Sun" appeared first in *Other Islands*; "Learning Sex from the Dictionary" appeared first in *Gathering Place of the Waters: Thirty Milwaukee Poets*; "The Secret" appeared first in *The Louisville Review*; and "Footsteps" appeared first in *Abraxas*.

BONNIE FISHER (poems, p. 256) grew up silent in St. Paul, Minnesota. In the past six years she has discovered writing as a powerful means of exploring and giving voice to her life.

TOM HANSEN (poems, p. 155) teaches at Northern State College in Aberdeen, South Dakota. His poems and book reviews and occasional articles about teaching and doing poetry writing appear from time to time in various little magazines and literary journals. The poems included here are based on drawings by his two sons, Paul and Christopher. "The Man in the Moon's Loony Brother" first appeared in *Kansas Quarterly*; "God" first appeared in *Tempo* (of course); and "In Olden Days" and "The Faces of the Cook" first appeared in *Milkweed Chronicle*.

MARGARET HASSE (poems, p. 121) has published poetry in *Milkweed Chronicle, Tendril, Primavera, and 25 Minnesota Poets.* She was one of the winning poets in the Loft's Mentor Series in 1982. In 1983, she collaborated with two other writers on a play, *Sign of a Child*, for the Women's Theatre Project. Recently, she was a participant in *Secret Traffic*, an innovative theatre project which staged four writers in a performance. "Light in the Head" first appeared in *Northeast* and "Heat Lightning" in *Great River Review*.

SUSAN HAUSER (poems, p. 126) was born in Minneapolis in 1942. She has an MFA from Bowling Green State University (Ohio) and is editor/publisher of Raspberry Press. She is a free-lance writer and author of how-to books. She lives within mosquito range of a wonderful floating bog in northern Minnesota. "How, Like This Spring, Slowly" first appeared in *Woman Poet*, "Night Class: Petit Point" in *Sing Heavenly Muse!*, and "Hair Combing" in *Loonfeather*.

JOEL HELGERSON (fiction, p. 211) was born in Winona, Minnesota in 1950 and graduated from the University of Minnesota with a B.A. in American Studies. Since college he has resided throughout the Midwest and West and is currently employed as a technical writer in Minneapolis. "Tulips" was originally published in *Fallout*.

SARA HUNTER (poems, p. 82), a native Minnesotan and Macalester College graduate, holds a Ph'D in clinical psychology from the University of Minnesota. She has also studied in Japan, Italy, and Austria. She has been a science writer and managing editor for Harper and Row and a senior psychologist at the Ramsey County Mental Health Center, working with abused children who become frequent studies of her poetry. She is currently in private practice in St. Paul and specializes in adult and family counseling. She has authored many poems and professional articles.

PATRICIA HUTCHINGS (poems, p. 180) was born and reared in Iowa and has spent most of her life in the midwest. For the past six years she has lived in Milwaukee, Wisconsin, where she is chair of the English Department at Alverno College. In addition to her normal teaching duties there, she is currently directing a college-wide campaign to promote creativity in all disciplines. "Auden and the Animals" first appeared in *The Chowder Review* and "Anagnorisis" in *Gathering Place of the Waters: 30 Milwaukee Poets*, edited by Bill Lueders (Gathering Place Productions, 1983).

MARCIA JAGODZINSKE (poems, p. 102) lives in Brainerd, Minnesota. She says of her work, "I have been writing longer than I haven't been. You might say it's my life's blood. You might not. My poetry is published throughout the United States and Canada."

ELIZABETH ANN KNIGHT (poems, p. 267) says of herself, "I am a gardener who has done many other kinds of work. I've lived in New England, Germany, upstate New York, Oregon, and at last Minnesota. My parents sprang from the Midwest and that may account for my arrival and settling." "Dakota Homestead, 1879" first appeared in *Sing Heavenly Muse!*, "John Runk, Photographs, 1912" in *The Lake Street Review*, and "Two for Mary" in *Harbinger*.

MARGOT FORTUNATO KRIEL (poems, p. 172) grew up in South Carolina and came to the Midwest in the late '60's. She holds a Ph'D in American Studies from the University of Minnesota. She teaches creative writing and women's studies, and writes feature articles about the arts, medicine, and other subjects. Her poems have appeared in *Milkweed Chronicle*, *Sing Heavenly Muse!*, *The Iowa Review*, and elsewhere, and she contributed to the anthology *The Selby Lake Bus: Six Minneapolis-St. Paul Poets* in 1979. She lives just off Summit Avenue in St. Paul with her daughter Helena.

NORITA DITTBERNER LARSON (poems, p. 25) has been writing poetry for eight years. She is a member of the poetry group, Onionskin, and a frequent contributor to *WARM Journal*. She is a Montessori teacher and the author of six books for children published by Creative Education. She lives in St. Paul, Minnesota. "Family Reunion 1950" and "Photograph in Yesterday's Paper" first appeared in *Sing Heavenly Muse!* and "West Seventh" first appeared in *WARM Journal*.

CARL LINDNER (poems, p. 34) has had two chapbooks published: *Vampire* (1977) and *The Only Game* (1981). *Shooting Baskets in a Dark Gymnasium*, his first full-length collection of poems, will be coming out from Linwood Publishers in April 1984. He has a "passion for chocolate and hot Chinese food."

SUE ANN MARTINSON (poems, p. 97) is the editor of *Sing Heavenly Muse!*, a Minneapolis-based literary journal of women's poetry and prose. "Allegro Risoluto" first appeared in *Onion Skin*.

WILLIAM MEISSNER (fiction, p. 197) directs the creative writing program at St. Cloud State University. He has had twelve stories published in ten magazines including *The Indiana Review*, *Great River Review*, and *Gallimaufrey*. *Learning to Breathe Underwater* (his first full-length collection of poems) was published by Ohio University Press in 1980. He won a PEN/NEA Syndicated Fiction Award in 1983 (with a story published in *The Minneapolis Sunday Star & Tribune* and in other newspapers). He has been a winner of the Loft/McKnight Award (1982), an NEA Fellowship in Writing (1973), and a grant from the Minnesota State Arts Board (1982). He lives with his wife and son in St. Cloud, Minnesota.

MARY VIRGINIA MICKA (poems, p. 145) is a member of the Congregation of the Sisters of St. Joseph and teaches writing and literature at the College of St. Catherine in St. Paul, Minnesota. She has received awards from The Poetry Group of Utica, from the White Bear Lake Writers, and in *The Southern Poetry Review*, National Competition. Her work has been accepted by *Indiana Writes*, *The New Yorker*, and *The Southern Poetry Review*. In 1983, she was one of four Twin Cities poets performing their work in "Secret Traffic," a theatre piece sponsored by the Loft in Minneapolis. "Small Things Tell Us," "Rinse O White," and "My House" were included in that performance.

DONNA NITZ MULLER (fiction, p. 107) was born in Sioux Falls, South Dakota and graduated from Mount Marty College in Yankton where she studied writing. She also studied with J. Hemesath at the Dakota Writer's Conference. She has had fiction published in *Iowa Woman*. She is married and has six children. She lives with her family in Salem, South Dakota.

ANDREA MUSHER (poems, p. 248) says of herself: "I support my habit of writing poetry by teaching in colleges, prisons, and nursing homes. I hold degrees from Cornell University and the University of Wisconsin-Madison. Currently I am exploring the cultural artifacts of Southern California while attempting to revive the power of the written word here in movie/video land." "Vacation Post Cards from the East Coast" first appeared in *Abraxas*.

JANE O'CONNELL NOWAK (fiction, p. 61) is a transplant from Massachusetts, where she sometimes taught high school English and sometimes practiced law. Currently, she spends holidays learning to write fiction and laughing, while living with her husband, Michael, in West St. Paul, Minnesota. She recently had her first story published in *The Lake Street Review*.

MARY FRANCOIS ROCKCASTLE (fiction, p. 11) grew up in New Jersey and has lived in Minneapolis, Minnesota for nine years. She has an M.A. in writing from the University of Minnesota. She works as a teacher of writing and as a free-lance writer. She was a recipient of a Bush Fellowship in 1983. She is married and has a four-year-old daughter. An earlier version of "Memories of a Maria Goretti Girl" appeared in *Fallout*.

NANCY ROTENBERRY (poems, p. 52) was born and still lives in St. Paul, Minnesota. She holds a B.A. from Macalester College in journalism and German, and an M.A. in English as a Second Language from the University of Minnesota, where she currently teaches composition to foreign students. She was an award winner in the 1981 Ruth Lusk Ramsey Poetry Contest, and has had her poetry set to music by Cary John Franklin (with several performances in the Janet Wallace Concert Hall at Macalester). She says that the Mille Lacs Lake cabin she shares with her husband and family is one of life's great pleasures.